Gift from

The Field

By
Dodie Meeks

Panther Creek Press

Spring, Texas

Copyright © 2002 by Darlene Ruth Meeks.
All rights reserved including the right of reproduction in whole or in part in any form

Published by Panther Creek Press
SAN 253-8520
116 Tree Crest, P.O. Box 130233
Panther Creek Station
Spring, TX 77393-0233

Cover painting by the author
Cover design by Adam Murphy
The Woodlands, TX

Manufactured in the United States of America
Printed and bound by DataDuplicators, Inc.
Houston, TX

1 2 3 4 5 6 7 8 9 10

Library of Congress Cataloguing in Publication Data

Meeks, Dodie

    The field

    I. Title   II. Fiction

ISBN 09718361-4-0

This novel is dedicated to my children, who learned what rotten parents writers are from watching me work on a typewriter in the middle of the playpen in their nursery, and still turned out to be far nicer adults than any mother could deserve.

I

"Some people listen. Some people wait," Peg said. "They're not the same." She blew her nose and mopped at her eyes. "You've got to be the best listener in Houston, Texas, the United States, world, universe, Mind of God."

Hetty Bach smiled. She was spending the entire afternoon of what would become the worst day of her life listening to Peg Albright, wishing her husband Peter would come home. Pete could be so good at commiserating. All Hetty could do was listen. It was a comfort to hear that Peg found that consoling.

Peg didn't cry like a middle-aged person. She cried in spurts and squalls, her eyes squirting tears. She'd worked her way through two boxes of Kleenex and Hetty had to go rummage around under the sink in the downstairs bathroom to find her a third. Peg's husband, Jerome, had walked out on her again, leaving her pregnant this time, with a couple of teen-age boys and a perfectly huge mortgage on a four-bedroom Sagemont house that needed to have the foundation repaired.

When Peg wasn't weeping and pregnant she had a star-shot smile that could stop a man in his tracks and make him wheel around and stare after her, swallowing to keep from drooling. She could flip that platinum hair back and smile at an escalator full of tired business men going down, down, down, and each man, as he came abreast of her, would light up and straighten his tie like it was Christmas day in the morning.

Peg would turn herself inside out for Hetty too, if Hetty ever needed to have someone turn herself inside out, but this long afternoon all she could do was rant and weep. And Hetty couldn't think why Pete had decided to disappear for hours and hours on a long holiday afternoon.

"Jerry says he needs to go find himself," Peg said, a damp Kleenex at her nose. "You believe that? I asked him if he had any idea where to go look. Like under a rock? And he said that was just the kind of thing he couldn't stand. And I said maybe he ought to look under Pamela or was she totally a missionary position person and he said at least Pamela wouldn't break anything if she ever did get on top."

"Oh, honey," Hetty said.

"Pamela shops at the Five, Seven and Nine," Peg said.

Hetty couldn't think what the Five, Seven and Nine was.

"It's that store in Baybrook Mall," Peg said. "With the clerks that look like concentration camp survivors, only young. Really young. About half Jerome's age."

"Dear."

"Yeah," Peg said. "She has a size two butt. We were supposed to have a loving family picnic today, Jerry promised the kids. Only the night before last I found this little note in his suit pocket with the Five, Seven and Nine card and the phone number with this cutesy heart on it around a note: 'Your little idiot'."

"Oh, honey," Hetty said.

"Yeah. His little idiot," Peg said. "He says it doesn't mean a thing." She hiccoughed. "That's what I used to be. His little idiot. Not lately, but you know."

Her voice wavered and broke and she was off again. "So last night he's all huggy and patty and I'm supposed to forget everything. 'Where's my honey bun?' he goes, and I lost it. 'At Forest Park East,' I told him. 'You're laid out in your black pinstripe and I'm in the front row in red satin cut all the way down to here.'

"'That so?' he goes. 'Yeah,' I said. 'And I'm laughing my head off.'"

She sniffed. "Like Julia Roberts. You know that big helpless laugh?" She threw back her head and brayed hoarsely.

Sounded dreadful. "Don't," Hetty said. "Gracious."

She couldn't help glancing up at the clock. Peter might have had car trouble or something but he always called. Always.

Peg slumped back and shoved her pale hair behind her ears. When she bowed her head, her hair slid forward again, veiling her face. "Do you think I've got Julia Roberts's mouth?"

"No," Hetty said. "You have your own mouth. But I happen to like Julia Roberts." She sighed. "Peter and I both like Julia Roberts. I wish I could remember where he said he was going."

"Big-mouthed.'" Peg went on, scowling. "So I've got a big mouth. I'm a big woman." She peered from under her eyebrows. "Oh, quit stewing about Pete. He'll be along. You're Jerome's type, you know. Petite. How many times have you heard Jerome on how lucky Pete is to have you?"

"Oh, please." Hetty restrained a shudder. Sleazy Jerome, for heaven's sake. "How about an English muffin?"

"No," Peg said, trying for hauteur. "Thank you."

"There's some of that marmalade from last summer."

"Oh, hell," Peg said. "Why not? Only aren't you getting ready to put that bread in the oven? Why don't I wait for that?" She paced carefully around Hetty's kitchen rocking chair and stopped to look at an unfinished collage on the easel in the corner opposite the big window. "Wish I could paint," she said. "Wish I could do something."

"Being a mother is something," Hetty said.

Peg wiped her eyes and came over to hug her. "I'm being a pain. Sorry. That's what you get, you bread baker person. My mom used to make bread. She said pounding the dough helped her to keep from pounding me."

Hetty flashed on Peg's mother, Leona, in an immaculate apron, bitterly slapping at a heap of white dough on an immaculate table, with her mouth in a tight white smile.

"Oh, Hetty," Peg said. "I had to tell my mom about all this. It was so awful." She pursed her lips and shook her head, doing an imitation: "'I hate to be negative, Margaret, but you can be very trying.'" She balled up a Kleenex and threw it at the wastebasket and pulled another one from the box. "'Trying.'"

Hetty nodded. She'd heard Leona say that a time or two.

She got up and opened the refrigerator. "Maybe some fruit? You want an apple? Apples are our friends."

Peg didn't even try for a smile. "No, thanks. It makes Jerry crazy, having the boys so nuts about Peter, you know. And it tears him up the way you two can't go anywhere, like the Mall, or anywhere, without kids running up acting like Pete is this celebrity:

'Mr. Bach, Mr. Bach.' His fans. You ever watch Jerry's face any time that happens?"

"All teachers get that," Hetty said.

"Yeah, I guess. Instead of pay, right?"

Hetty shrugged.

"How am I gonna make house payments?" Peg wailed. "We keep getting behind now." She tugged at her hair. "You know what's gonna happen. Oh, yeah, oh, yeah, I'm gonna be on my own, you better believe it. As soon as I'm single, I'll just have to find somebody. Who do we know who's single who wants three kids?"

She didn't expect an answer.

"Let's see," she went on, "There's fuzzy old Kent Cox, speaking of teacher's pay, but I'm not sure I could handle living with a guy who lets a dog sleep on the foot of his bed."

Hetty looked at her.

"Woof, woof," Peg said. "Milo has his own quilt and pillow. Besides, I'm not sure Kent likes kids. He can be sweet, though. He can be sort of like Roseanne's husband, the big teddy bear one. Don't you think?"

"No." Hetty sighed. "If you married Kent you'd have another boy to take care of."

Something kept prickling at the edge of her mind. She shivered and rubbed her arms. "Want me to fix a cup of tea? Hot tea, I mean. Hot is more comforting."

Peg wasn't listening. "Roseanne's husband," she said. "That type."

Hetty sighed. "Kent Cox is not a type," she said. "He's our Kent. Who loves us, whom we love, who happens to have a very nice black Labrador retriever." She knew better than to argue but when Peg got to typecasting she had to be stopped. David Gofor, across the street, bore no resemblance to Marvin Zindler, but Peg came up with that in front of a room full of people at a PTA meeting. When Peg was engaged to Jerome she insisted he was a dead ringer for Paul Newman, for heaven's sakes.

"Quit looking at the clock," Peg said. "He'll be along."

"I'm not," Hetty said. "I just wish he'd call. Is it getting too chilly in here?" She shivered.

"Jerome and I started dividing stuff up and I told him to take his damned recliners," Peg said. "The sofa looks kind of weird without 'em but who needs a two-recliner sofa? Did I ever ask for a two-recliner sofa?" She gazed at the ceiling, tears leaking out of her eyes. "What am I gonna do?" When she leaned forward, Hetty came across the room to rub her back.

"Ah," Peg said. "To the left. There. You know what? Pete probably won't even let himself die on you for fear you'll take a flying leap onto the funeral pyre. You won't even have to leap. You can just sort of slide down, since you two have been joined at the hip for...what? Fifteen years?"

"Eighteen," Hetty said, evenly. "I don't know as we're joined at the hip, exactly." She quit rubbing and walked back to stand gazing out at the driveway through the window above the sink. The sun had gone down. She gave an ivy a drink and closed the blinds in the little window and moved around, turning on lamps. She circled back to light the oven and set the timer.

"Like, Pete's in love with a fifty-seven Chevy," Peg was saying. "And lucky you, golly gee, what do you get to drive but a green and white fifty-seven Chevy. How many times have you had to walk home from Kroger's when that thing quit on you?"

Hetty shrugged. "Peter drives the Chevy, mostly. That may be what's keeping him." She moved back to sit down across the table from Peg. Shadow wove himself around her ankles and leaped to her lap. She picked him up and addressed him, nose to nose: "Boy, what some people don't know. That Chevy is the best car those people ever made."

Shadow didn't much care for being held nose to nose. As soon as she moved him to her lap he slid loose and stepped away, his tail in the air.

Hetty sighed. "Maybe I wouldn't exactly have chosen green and white," she said.

Peg snorted. "The only people I know who would deliberately choose a heap like Clara are demented delinquents. Of course, that's just jake with Saint Peter, isn't it?"

Hetty stiffened. "Well, since it would seem demented delinquents are the closest thing to his own children that Peter will ever have, that's probably just as well, isn't it?" she said, evenly.

Peg looked away. "Aw, hell," she said. "I'm sorry. I'm just

flailing around. But God, when did I ever pray for big clunky kids? You should have had a house full. They'd be really nice, with big gray eyes and lots of red hair and—"

"And a few gray streaks," Hetty said.

The oven sent out a faint, false, sweet scent. She got up and slid in four pans full of pale bloated dough and gently closed the oven door. "I'm thirty-five and Peter will be forty-four, next month."

"I know," Peg said. She honked into a Kleenex. "Thing is, you take in all of 'em. Even Dave and Louise's nerdy kid, across the street. Don't you ever get fed up with being the earth mother to half the delinquents at Dobie High?"

"No." Hetty glanced quickly, defensively, around at her blue and white open-shelved kitchen with its rows of copper pans. "A person could do worse," she said, and immediately thought, oh, poor Peg. She has to lash out at someone and here I am, all smug and cherished. "Peter and I lucked into each other before either of us knew beans. It was practically incest, as you know. We were pretty well acquainted. But even that was luck. Pure luck."

Peg sniffed. "Lucky you," she said. "Lucky Pete. What if his mom and dad had decided to rescue some rotten little bitch?"

"She wouldn't have stayed rotten, in that house," Hetty said. "Look. Why don't you go see if you can rescue the boys from Grandma Leona? Bring them over here and spend the night, tonight? We can get a movie and make some caramel corn."

"Ah, hell. The kids and my mom deserve each other," Peg said, wiping her eyes. "You have to help me figure out where I went wrong. Like, maybe I should have baked more bread," she said, hoarsely. She nodded at Hetty's easel, in the corner. "Or taken up water colors? Who needs a big boring blimp?"

Hetty glanced at the clock. Almost eight. Oh, Peter, she thought. Pick up the phone.

Poor Peg can't help being bitchy though. Anymore than Boots could.

Hetty contemplated her hands and drifted back, hearing her mother's bitter laugh, her voice echoing in that high-ceilinged house in Galveston. Boots. Such an unmotherly sounding name. Hetty's third grade teacher once told the class that the word "boot" came from "bot" meaning "toadish" or "squat" and had lapsed into consternation and unhappy confusion at Hetty's furious tears. "My mother isn't squat. She couldn't be squat. Ever."

She couldn't, either. Boots had coppery hair and ice blue eyes and she smelled of gardenias, all her lingerie and her satiny pillows smelled of gardenias, because Boots was Mrs. Lord. They were all Lords, George Gordon loved saying. She, Hetty, George Gordon's precious Heather Angel, was a Lord. "We are the Lords of Galveston," he'd say, "dwelling forever in the House of the Lord." He had a bronze plaque made for the sign on the post out in front that proclaimed that that was what their house was: "The House of the Lord." In Galveston's Silk Stocking District. With the crazy fire pole in the front hall, that George Gordon brought home from the fire station when they dismantled it, because he just knew that a brass fire pole belonged in their house and besides the city didn't have any use for that pole so it was a grand bargain. George Gordon loved grand bargains. "We're the only house on the Island with a fire pole," he exulted.

Boots loathed the fire pole. Not that that had anything to do with her leaving. For the longest time, Hetty had been so sure that Boots had gone away because of something she, Hetty, did or didn't do, in her bungling way, with her endless attempts to keep things on an even keel in that creaking old Victorian house. The house of the Lord had a parquet foyer, where Hetty learned to roller skate; a wide, curving banister, that she learned to balance on, all the way down; a narrow, dark, worn, back stair that wound up from the kitchen into a narrow hall on the third floor off what had once been a ballroom, where she could huddle and listen and worry.

Sometimes Boots would find her and announce, exasperated, "We are expecting people. Darling, can't you do something about yourself? Have you been chewing on your sash? Where's your father?" which meant that Hetty ought to try to do something about making George Gordon be somehow different, but Hetty couldn't think what that difference might be. Boots was not very specific. "Don't be draggy, darling," she'd say, "lighten up," languidly derisive, waving one of her filter tipped slender cigarettes. Hetty's very presence was an affront, with her freckles and her forever coming loose braids and her socks working down into the heels of her shoes.

Poor George Gordon. Her big, sweet, genial dad never seemed

to realize that they were living in a world where the lights would be turned off if a check weren't mailed or that strangers would storm in to take the furniture away if he didn't do something. Hetty didn't realize how difficult that could be until after Boots was gone.

"Where'd you go?" Peg was demanding.

Hetty shook her head and stood up and walked over to look in the refrigerator. "Just reminiscing, I guess. Sorry. You want some water?" She got out the pitcher and brought a couple of glasses to the table. "My dad used to call my mother his 'gorgeous witchy bitch,'" she said. "It was one of his pet endearments. I used to worry about that." She grinned ruefully. "I worried about everything. Must have been such a joy, to live with." She sighed.

"Well," Peg said. "George Gordon."

"Oh, come on," Hetty said. "Tell you what. As long as your boys are all set, you're staying right here, tonight. Pete and I aren't going to let you go home by yourself, you know that." She glanced at the clock. Almost nine. Why didn't Pete call? He always called. "Wish I could remember where he said he was off to."

"Joined at the hip," Peg said, bitterly. "So maybe if I'd shined Jerry's shoes and...and...cut his hair? That's it. It's all your fault. Maybe I should have borrowed your hair clippers?"

"Enough," Hetty said. "All this can't be good for the baby."

But Peg couldn't quit. "If I could have stuck to the grapefruit diet, maybe? Look at you, though, you never diet and you're the same size you were when you got married. Is that fair?" She was starting to sob, again. "That's another damned thing—"

"Peggy, enough!" Hetty said. "You look just the way you are supposed to. Nice and round and womanly. And you've always had lovely skin and lovely soft hair and after you've had this perfectly lovely baby you'll be yourself, again. And I am not either the same. Nothing the matter with a little padding. Covers the nerves."

"Yeah, right," Peg said, getting up. "You know what? I ought to feel good. I mean, how long does a bank robber or a murderer serve? And here I've put in all these years with all that lousy sex and—" She glanced up at Hetty and her mouth snapped shut. She slid down into her chair with a thump. "What?"

"I don't know." Hetty shivered. She stood up and hugged herself. "Something's wrong. Just hold it, a minute."

"What?" Peg's eyes were round.

"Give me a minute," Hetty said, wincing. She walked over to stand with her hands flat on the table, bracing herself. "There's...something. Something's awfully wrong." She swallowed. She couldn't explain. She had to sit down. All she knew was that something was sickening her. Her ears had started to ring. A clammy chill rode all along her veins. "Give me a minute," she gasped. "Aren't you cold? It's freezing in here."

2

"What is it?" Peg asked.

Hetty shivered. She couldn't answer. She felt the way she had on that ghastly afternoon when Peter's mother and dad died in that accident on the Gulf Freeway. Both of them gone, killed, Peter's mom and dad, who had become her parents by then, truly the truest parents Hetty had ever known, suddenly gone, both of them. She didn't want to think about it.

She was still chilled and queasy, Peg was repeatedly demanding to know what was the matter, when the front door bell chimed. There were two men out on the front stoop. One of them, tall and so soft-spoken that he was almost hard to understand, introduced himself as Thomas Gray, Lieutenant Tom Gray. "May we come in?" he asked. "This is Lieutenant Stephens. We have some unhappy news, I'm afraid." Neither man could meet Hetty's eyes. The older of the two detectives, Lieutenant Stephens, looked so distressed—his trousers rippled on his legs—that Hetty started to shake and could hardly breathe.

"It's about Peter," Hetty said. "Come in. Tell me. Where is he?"

"Afraid so, ma'am," Lieutenant Gray said. The men came in but they didn't sit down. Lieutenant Gray wanted Hetty to sit down. He talked about somebody hitting somebody, his voice so low, so haltingly unhappy, that Hetty could hardly hear him, let alone comprehend. "He's unconscious? Where? Which hospital?"

"Memorial Southeast. We could take you there, if you like."

"It's bad, isn't it?" Peg said.

The detective looked at the carpet and when he lifted his eyes, his face looked so drawn that Hetty's ears started to ring. She could hardly hear him. "I'm afraid Mr. Bach is not conscious."

The Field

Hetty swallowed. "I don't understand. Oh, never mind. We can talk at the hospital, can't we?"

"Certainly," Lieutenant Gray said. He glanced around. "Is something cooking? You wouldn't want to leave the stove on. You might want to sit down for a few minutes, Mrs. Bach."

The man wasn't making sense. He stood gazing down at her, his shoulders hunched all the way up to his ears, lifting and dropping his hands, making helpless calming motions. "Sit down?" Hetty's couldn't understand. "Was anyone else hurt?"

"The bread," Peg said, swallowing a sob. "I'll get it."

"It's not done," Hetty said. "Oh, leave it. Turn off the oven and just leave it. Peg, Peggy, Peter's been in an accident. I knew it. I just knew it." She hated crying in front of people, in front of these strangers and Peg. Peg had stopped crying now. Peg was handing her the box of tissues, staring at her, her face blotchy and pale. "You mustn't be sick," Hetty told her. "Could you not be sick, please?"

Peg drove to Southeast Memorial.

The detectives caught up with Hetty and Peg outside the emergency room entrance. A nurse wouldn't let Hetty go through a pair of swinging doors to try to find Peter. When she tried to edge past the woman she was stopped by the taller of the two detectives, Lieutenant Gray. He enveloped Hetty, turned her around, and, when she resisted, said he knew how she felt, and she was right, she was absolutely right, but why didn't they go find a place to sit quietly for a couple of minutes. She let him tuck her arm in his and lead her down the hall to a small room.

Peg sat beside her, miserable and silent, as the lanky detective sat down and stood up and sat down again, suggesting everybody relax.

The small room had a glass topped table with three battered magazines and a small clay pot with a dying African violet in it. The clay pot was tied with a paper ribbon. After several minutes, Peg peeled the ribbon from the pot and sat winding and unwinding it around her fingers, asking if anyone wanted any coffee. She said she was pretty sure there had to be coffee somewhere near.
No one wanted any coffee.

"As long as we're having to wait," Hetty said, "I want to know exactly what happened." She drew in a deep breath. "If you please."

The lanky detective, Lieutenant Gray, made a visible effort at bracing himself. "Yes, well, you have to realize that what we've got here isn't an accident, exactly," he said. "Three teenagers saw what looked like a fight."

"A fight?" Hetty had to overcome a small snort of disbelief as she tried to explain. "Peter? Oh, Peter wouldn't begin to know how to—a fight? With fists?"

The man explained, choosing his words carefully, "Three teenagers saw what appeared to be an attack." He took in a breath. "On your husband."

Hetty shook her head. "I don't understand." Her clenched hands were hurting her mouth. "Someone struck Peter?"

"Slugged him," the older detective, Lieutenant Stephens, took over. "The witnesses say it looked like a fight. This is difficult, but we have to ask. Do you know of anyone who would attack your husband for any reason?"

The very idea was so preposterous that Hetty couldn't begin to grasp it. "Someone struck Peter down? With his fists?" She shuddered. "And that was enough to hurt him so badly? How can that be? And now he's unconscious. I don't understand. But he may not be unconscious much longer." She looked toward the doorway of the room.

"He was thrown against the tailgate of a truck," Lieutenant Stephens said. "The assailant drives a red Ford pickup truck. He's a large man, dark-haired, possibly a student at Dobie High School?"

Hetty couldn't help making a small derisive sound. "None of this makes sense. No. No, I don't know of anyone who would want to fight with Peter. He's never had a fist fight in his life."

"Possibly a student, Mrs. Bach." The man went on. "We have to ask these things. The sooner we're briefed, the more likely it is that we can locate this person, this student, if he is a student. A student with an old red pickup truck. The witnesses think he might be a Bandido. A motorcycle gangster."

"In a red pickup truck, " Peg said.

"I don't know," Hetty said. "I don't know. Oh, this is insane." She got up and picked up the dead plant on the glass table top and walked over to drop it into a wastebasket in the corner of the room.

The Field

The tall detective's face darkened in disapproval. "This may not be the time, Steve."

The older detective shrugged and picked up one of the battered magazines.

Peg got up from the sofa and faced both the men, her hands on her hips. "Some of those kids aren't too crazy about Peter at the beginning of the year, but by Memorial Day most of them are ready to join the fan club," she said. "Even the Bandidos and the Kings and the rest of the gangsters come around. Pete's been teaching for a quarter of a century, for gosh sakes. He's like some kind of an icon to those kids."

Hetty said, fighting tears. "Peter won the Golden Apple. This past year. Again."

The detectives glanced at each other. Lieutenant Stephens said, "Well. The man was in a red pickup. A Mazda. Or a Ford. An old truck. If that rings any bells."

"Oh, ding, dong, ding," Peg glared at the man. "If that rings any bells." She sat down and took Hetty's hand in hers. "A red pick-'em-up truck," she said, tearfully bright-eyed, with a small bitter laugh, "My husband, Jerome, has a red pickup. But he's no slugger. Dave Gofor had one but he's a pencil pusher if ever you want to see one. I think the automotive teacher, Kent Cox, donated his red pickup to those kids to work on in class." She was counting on her fingers and lost track. "Then there's, let's see. Hell, half the men in Houston have pickups and most of them are red. George Gordon used to drive a red pickup and, like I said, Hetty's neighbors across the street, the Gofor family, used to have one up at the lake, but it died, and the—"

"Peg. Please," Hetty murmured, "Talk less." She turned to the tall detective in time to see his lips twitch and the lines around his eyes crinkle in what might have been a faint smile.

"Ma'am?" he said.

"I know a good many of Peter's students," Hetty told him. "Especially the ones with difficulties. But I can't think of anyone who would hurt him. These witnesses, I assume they're students as well?"

The detective nodded. "We've been talking with them. We'll be going around to talk with them and with their parents later tonight."

"I see," Hetty said. She hesitated. "What misery, all around."

"Oh, look at her," Peg said, her voice going shrill. She got up and began to pace. "Why doesn't somebody tell us what's happening? Isn't somebody going to get around to telling us what's going on around here, sooner or later?"

The tall detective turned to Hetty. He's trembling again, she thought. He looked toward the doorway of the room and a look of such dread washed over his face that she knew what he was thinking.

"You're wrong," she whispered. She cleared her throat. "They might be coming to tell us that he's revived. That he's waking up, wondering what happened."

The man couldn't answer her.

Then he was answering her. He was shaking his head, sorrowing, moving his head back and forth in a slow and definite response. "I'm so sorry," he said. "Oh, Mrs. Bach. I am so very sorry."

3

Memorial Day night, sixteen-year-old Donald Gofor was hunched in his dad's leather recliner in front of the bay window in the Gofor's living room, watching the front of the Bach's house across the street. He was waiting to see if Aunt Hetty might come back with those detectives and Mrs. Albright. He figured she was probably spending the night at the hospital, sitting next to Mr. Bach's bed. Or identifying the body, maybe. Standing behind a pane of glass, watching some guy slide a drawer out of a cooler, like on TV, only for real, with Mr. Bach on it, on this slab, with his head bashed in.

That guy really slugged him.

Slammed him into the back of that truck.

Knocked his brains out.

Donald kept going over it and going over it, wishing he hadn't seen it, wishing he could get past it enough to think about something else for a couple of minutes at a time. He had the TV going with the sound off.

He just kept wondering how Mr. Bach was doing.

Like he didn't know. He knew, all right. He and Gilly and Bill. Bill and Gilly hadn't seemed too torn up about it, but they didn't know Aunt Hetty and Mr. Bach the way Donald did. All his life. Better than he knew anybody. A hell of a lot better than he knew his dad, for instance.

When he first got home, Donald had thought about calling his dad and mother to tell them about the whole thing. "Guess what, Gilly and Bill and I just saw Mr. Bach get slugged and he's got to be dead or dying because I think I saw his brains coming out of his head." But he figured it would keep. The guys were with him and Donald didn't feel like sitting around in front of them, talking to his mother and his dad at his mom's company's Memorial Day party. Donald couldn't see himself trying to explain it on the phone, his dad telling him to make it quick, standing around balancing the receiver with a drink and his cigarette, and his mother, half looped, telling him that's nice, Donald, dear, it's a little noisy here, dear. Telling him she'd be home soon, and couldn't it wait?

He just wanted to sit here by himself, Donald was thinking, when the two detectives rang the front doorbell. Donald wasn't surprised. He and Gilly and Bill had gone over the whole thing with the cops out next to the field and over it again with these same two lieutenants about eight or ten times, it seemed like, but they said they'd be coming by, and here they were. For some routine follow up, they said.

The tall one, Lieutenant Gray, apologized for bothering him, late as it was. Donald said that was okay. The two of them came in and sat down on the sofa. Donald turned off the TV. They didn't want any Cokes or potato chips.

"How's Mister Bach doing?" Donald asked. Like he didn't know. "You think he's gonna make it?"

"He's badly hurt," Lieutenant Gray said.

"How's Aunt Hetty?" Donald heard how that sounded and explained, fast, that she wasn't his aunt, that's what he called her. What he used to call her. "She used to baby sit me and Doris," he explained. "How's she doing?"

"She's a brave lady," the lieutenant said.

Then the other one, Lieutenant Stephens, asked if they might be disturbing his parents. That struck Donald funny but he explained and sighed and got ready to go over the whole thing again.

Donald said the thing was that he felt rotten for not doing something to help Mr. Bach. "It happened so fast," he said. The two men looked at him like they knew what else. What else was that he and the guys were scared shitless.

Lieutenant Stephens asked the first question. "The three of you." He consulted his notes, and had Donald spell out Gilly's full name, Dwayne Gilbreath and Bill's, William Wadsworth Chaney. Donald went and got his address book to be sure of their addresses, before the detective went on. "Mister Gilbreath was at the wheel?"

"Yes, sir. We were in Gilly's Nissan Stanza. It's a ninety-two," Donald said. "White. Which is why I think the Dutchman might have seen us."

"Yes, well," the detective said. "Let's get back to the beginning, here. You and Mister Gilbreath and Mister Chaney were, what? Out for a drive?"

"That's right," Donald said. "Sir. Just, you know, cruising around." He didn't want to go into the cruising part of it too much. The detective had his eyebrows up. A lot of wild stuff went on over on that stretch of Telephone Road but he and the guys weren't into drugs or any of the rest of that. Well. Maybe they were kind of curious about the women. Gilly was, anyway. To hear him tell it. But Donald didn't really want to talk about that.

"We got tired of messing around tossing basketballs and watching Gilly's dad fool around with the brisket and decided to take off," he said. "Cruising. You know."

The detectives looked like they knew.

"Bill was in the front with Gilly," Donald said. "But I spotted the car."

He could still see it. Mr. Bach's green and white fifty-seven Chevy, parked next to this ratty field, with Mr. Bach out there, standing next to this rusted out, red pickup and the Dutchman slamming out of the truck, coming around with his head down.

The tall detective had this sadly patient smile. He said, "You were the one who saw the car?" and looked at Donald, waiting for him to go on.

"We were going on past," Donald said. "I yelled at Gilley to turn around. He pulled a U-turn. We came back slow, and Gilly pulled over and I saw him, I swear to God, the Dutchman, arguing with Mister Bach out in that field, crowding him. Getting up in his face. The Dutchman had, like, his head down." Donald demonstrated, his chin on his chest.

"Ah hah," the detective said. "The Dutchman. That's a street name, of course."

"Yes, sir." Donald swallowed. "His real name's Clifford. Clifford Van Huys. But you better not call him that."

"Ah, yes," the detective said. "Mister Van Huys."

"We call him the Dutchman," Donald said. "He looks at you, you call him whatever."

The detective glanced at his partner. "Your friends aren't so certain that's the man they saw," he said. "Pretty dark out there, wasn't it?"

Donald shrugged. "I guess. But that was him. I even think I saw this kind of a glint on his hand. The Dutchman's got this skull ring. I bet it left a mark on Mr. Bach. I've been thinking about that."

"The ring, yes." The detective sighed. "How close were you?"

"We kind of stayed on the shoulder of the road," Donald said. "But I know what I saw. Looked like he was shoving at him. Yelling." He shook his head in disbelief. "Yelling at Mister Bach."

"And?"

"And then he shoved him up against this truck and drew back and slugged him. Let him have it, man, right in the gut, and came back up under his chin in an uppercut. Picked Mister Bach up off the ground. He kind of lifted up, slammed back against the truck and slid down."

Donald could hear the shake in his voice. He was beginning to think the detective didn't realize what that was like, seeing that. "We shoulda done something," he said. "But it went so fast." Amazing how fast the whole thing went, him sitting in the back seat, Gilly slowing down and him, Donald, thinking *don't slow down, Gilly, God, keep going, come on,* hearing, like in the distance, Bill squeaking, "Let's go, man," and Gilly just sitting there, with the Dutchman looking down at Mr. Bach, socking his fist into his hand, his head swinging forward like he might look up, any minute.

The detectives listened, blank-faced.

It got quiet.

After a couple of minutes, Donald got to feeling like somebody ought to say something. "I think maybe there might have been a wreck started the whole thing, don't you?" he said. "You know, an accident, like?"

The men didn't say anything.

"Because the Dutchman kind of dragged himself along the side of the truck toward the door, at the last there, as we were pulling out."

"So you saw the assailant limp?"

"Yes, sir. Had to be road rage, don't you think?" Donald shook his head. "Some kind of rage."

The Field

"Then the three of you had a clerk at a grocery call nine-one-one," the detective said, reading from his notes. "Someone at that H.E.B. Food Pantry store?"

"Right," Donald said. "That was the nearest phone. Nobody had a cell phone. Man, it got wild."

Gilly burned rubber. He took the Beltway, ran the stop sign on the feeder, tore into the lot at the H.E.B. on Sabo and all three of them went barreling into the store, yelling at the woman in the courtesy booth to call the cops.

Then they drove back to the field.

Got back as the cops came pulling up, sirens and flashers, two Houston blue and whites and, in just a little while, the ambulance and a fire truck. Then a couple of minutes after that there was a sheriff's car, Harris County, white with those new gold reflectives.

"There was all this blood coming out of Mister Bach's nose and mouth," Donald said. "And you could see, maybe, his brains, when they picked him up. Boy. The medics took one look and hustled out a gurney and went 'one, two, three' and got him loaded up and got out of there." He was beginning to kind of wish the detectives would contribute to the conversation. "Sure you don't want a Coke?"

"No, thanks. There seems some dispute about the truck," the tall detective said.

"It was a Ford," Donald said. "Bill thought he got a partial on the plate."

"A partial?"

"Part of the number, maybe," Donald said. "But it was dark, sir, like you say. And Gilly's sure it's a Mazda. But it's a Ford. Gilly thinks he's this big expert. He always thinks that. We call him 'the answer man.' But we used to have a Ford pickup up at the lake house, so I know a Ford when I see it." Donald thought for a minute. "Like he doesn't think it was the Dutchman. The Dutchman's a pachuco, but y'all know about him, I guess. He's about twenty and he's still going to Dobie High."

"Slow down," the man said. "Take it easy."

"He's got all these Bandido buddies. With the Harleys? He's straight up wrong, man. He's probably got a rap sheet."

"A rap sheet?" The man smiled.

"Well, whatever you call it," Donald said, embarrassed. "Sir. Nobody messes with him, is what I'm saying. Well. Mister Bach, maybe."

"I see." The detective glanced at the windows. When he turned back to Donald he was frowning through a kind of a tired smile. "You're certain it was Mister Van Huys you saw?"

"The Dutchman slugged Mister Bach." Donald said. "He's some kind of a chief or whatever, I guess you know, in the Nomads. They're, like, the enforcers for the gang. He's got this Bandido headquarters over on Sageswept. The corner of Sageswept and Sageseason. One one twelve. It's a two-story. You probably got a file on that house. You got to have had a bunch of complaints from the neighbors. They hate all those Harleys."

He knew he was talking too much and he could hear how he was beginning to sound croaky but he had to keep trying to make them see. "He's got this mother supposed to live in Mexico someplace and his dad is somewhere nobody knows where, and he's got this big Harley. You going to pick him up? You ask me, you better pick him up, sirs, because if you don't, I got a gut feeling he saw us. Gilly's Stanza is, well, the Dutchman's got to know Gilly's Stanza. It's kind of beat up and he's got these bumper stickers."

The lieutenant ran his hand over his face, like he thought Donald might be getting carried away. What he wanted to talk about was the license plate thing. Again. Like anybody could see any numbers out in the dark.

Donald didn't know anything about any numbers. He said they should talk to Bill.

"And then?"

"Then we came on back here to my house," Donald said. "We stood around looking at the Bach's house, across the street, right out of this window here," and he flashed back to Gilly and Bill, standing around, peering through the blinds, sucking on Cokes and rehashing the whole thing.

He could hear Gilly, so excited his voice was going soprano on him, saying, "How long you think it'll take the cops to get over there to tell Miz Bach?"

"Looks peaceful, doesn't it?" Bill said. "That ain't gonna last." The lights were on in the Bach's house across the street. It looked

The Field

like always, white and peaceful under the street light, with this trimmed hedge in front and the Magnolia tree in bloom and the lawn green and smooth, knife-edged along the front curb with beds of white and yellow flowers lining the front walk and in neat little circles of mulch around the tall pines in the front yard.

"Wonder what they'll say," Gilly said. "The detectives, I mean. How they'll put it."

"Better them than me," Bill said. "She's got to take it hard."

"Yeah," Donald murmured. "Aunt Hetty." He sighed. When Gilly turned around with one eyebrow up he shrugged, embarrassed. "That's what we call her. Doris and me. To be polite." Then he got to thinking how Aunt Hetty acted like it was so great any time he showed up over there. Always had something good, like this cake made out of whipped cream and cookies he helped her put together, or banana-nut bread. She let Doris use her watercolor brushes for her social studies poster, that time. Donald's mother said those tubes of watercolor paints cost a fortune but Aunt Hetty didn't care. She squeezed out big blobs of paint and stood there watching, turning to look at him over fat Doris's shoulder with this slow smile, with her reddish hair twisted up with some of it coming loose around her face, paint spatters all over the place, all three of them happy as hell in that good-smelling kitchen.

"She's this really nice person," he said. "An artist and all."

"An artist?"

"Got this drawer so full of blue ribbons you can't get it shut." Donald wished Gilly would back off. "She's halfway famous."

"Well, don't bawl about it," Gilly said.

Donald shot him a look and said not to worry about it.

"Get a grip, man," Gilly said, starting to get kind of a snotty grin. The street light coming through the slats of the blind striped his long nose. Really showed up the zits around his mouth and sparkled off the braces.

"You ought to brush your teeth once in a while," Donald said. "Move over, man."

Gilly swung around and looked him over and looked at Bill, real quick, to see whose side Bill might be on, like if Bill might be getting ready to horse around with Donald or anything. But when he saw the look on Bill's face, Gilly looked back at Donald and said, totally on Donald's side, "Well, shit. Mister Bach, after all. Damn, huh?"

And Bill said, "Yeah. Damn." And the tight place in Donald's throat got tighter.

"You wanna go over there?" Bill said.

Donald shook his head. "No way in hell."

He and Gilly and Bill stood around looking at the house on the corner over there with Aunt Hetty inside it somewhere, maybe drawing or painting on one of those big thick sheets of watercolor paper, in the den over there. Humming under her breath, maybe. Walking around in her kitchen. Maybe polishing the copper pans hanging up all over the place in that kitchen or maybe getting out some cat food. Talking to Shadow like she did, just happy as hell, with no way of knowing she was about to hear the worst thing she ever could hear in her life any minute.

The detectives were looking at him.

"Sorry," Donald said. "I was just thinking. About Miz Bach. You know. Did you have to tell her? How did she take it?" She probably fell right down on the floor, he thought. It made him feel kind of queasy. "Is she at the hospital somewhere? As soon as they get home, I'm going to have to tell my mother and father where."

The tall detective rubbed his hand over his chin and down his neck to the open collar of his shirt. "She's in the waiting room of the intensive care unit," he said. He stood up and looked at his partner. "We through here, Steve?"

His partner shrugged. Both men thanked Donald. They went out and got in their car, took off down the wet gray street, their taillights disappearing before they rounded the corner on Sabo. The streetlights had misty halos. An owl screeched from the thicket at the Hike and Bike Trail. Donald closed and locked the front door and went and rummaged around in the pantry. He found a box of Saltines and a jar of pimento cheese. He took the cheese and crackers and another Coke into the front room, popped the top, settled himself in the recliner, and turned the TV back on. Paid programming on almost every channel. He found a rerun of M.A.S.H., sat and watched Hawkeye and B.J. kid around, making like surgeons, until he dozed off, the eerie scream of the owl riding around in him with the giggles and whoops of the TV laugh track.

4

It seemed a very long while before anyone came into the chilly little waiting room to tell Hetty and Peg very much of anything. A nurse said that a physician would come in as soon as one was free.

Peg was beside herself and Hetty was trying to convince her to go on home by the time a sad-eyed jowly little surgeon in green scrubs came looking for her. "Mrs. Bach?" he said in a rapid clipped accent. "I'm Doctor Ramesh. Would you come with me, please?"

Peg stood up, looked at him and sat back down. "I'll wait here."

The surgeon offered Hetty his arm as they walked down the hall and into an office. He indicated that she was to sit on a sofa. He pulled up a chair, facing her. He gazed into her face and hesitated, his mouth pulled down, shaking his head.

Oh, he looks so tired, she thought.

Then he began to speak and she had to concentrate to comprehend his staccato, British, Indian delivery. "Mrs. Bach, I must be honest. I believe you know your husband is badly injured? Yes. Badly. I cannot pretend things are going well." He hesitated. "At this point it is too early to be sure of anything." He sighed and hesitated again. His eyes were so dark they seemed all pupil, very liquid. The light from a small table lamp was reflected in them as he leaned toward her. He went on, rapidly, "The brain is damaged. Severely. Mister Bach is as stable as we are able to get him for the time being but he has been deeply unconscious since he arrived."

He paused and smiled, tremulously. "Ah," he said, "one of the paramedics who brought him in seems to know of Mister Bach. And one of the nurses, as well. This is most unusual in such a very large city, is it not? Mister Bach must be a very good man."

Hetty nodded. "But badly injured," she whispered.

He said, "I don't discuss odds. I won't say he has a ten per cent chance or some such thing because, right now, we really have no way to tell these things. Mrs. Bach, you need to hope for the best but you must be prepared for the worst. It is most unlikely that Mister Bach will survive. He will not regain consciousness." He sighed. "Dreadful," he said. "A dreadful thing."

When he stood up, Hetty got up, too, shakily, and thanked him, though she wasn't sure that he heard her. "May I see him?"

"Of course." The surgeon grimaced. "You are prepared? There is the respirator, of course. We're doing his breathing but his heart is beating on its own." He closed his eyes, briefly. "I've seen people pull through in some very extreme cases. I have. But your husband has very little brain function. I can assure you that he will be very well cared for. Right now, you should try to get some rest. We will call you if there is any change." He had on white shoes. A small bloody piece of something lay on the top of one of the laces. It looked like one of those little pieces of white rubbery meat that sometimes turn up in ground sirloin, that a person has to discard. Hetty tried not to keep looking down at it.

"I want to see him," Hetty said.

"Of course. Now, we wait. It would be well for you to get whatever rest you can."

After they got back to the little waiting room he said, quietly, to both Hetty and Peg, "Pray, if that's what you do. If it helps. Prayer does help some people."

But you don't think it will help Peter, do you? Hetty thought. You have to be wrong.

She looked at Peg through a blur of tears. Peg's eyes squeezed shut and opened again. "Pray for strength, you mean?" she asked.

"Something like that," the surgeon agreed. "I'm afraid so."

"Or for a miracle," Peg said, not making it a question.

The surgeon winced. "I'm afraid that's exactly the case."

"You don't believe in miracles," Hetty said, swallowing tears.

"Anything is possible," he said, quickly. "I wish you could have heard the staff talking about your husband, Mrs. Bach. I'm so sorry. He must be very good. Very good people." He repeated that as he led her into the intensive care unit. "Very good people."

Peter's head was cocooned in bandages. His poor face, what she could see of it, what wasn't covered by the bandages, was grotesquely swollen, the color of the curtains of his alcove. A small tubular triangle, absurdly like the musical instrument children play in kindergartens, hung suspended from a contraption over his head. She tried not to see the green plastic tubing snaking into his nose and mouth.

The respirator wheezed and whooshed. She sat down as close to the bars of the bed as she could get and took his cold hand in hers. One of his hands, the hand nearest her, was free of bandages. His fingers had what looked like dried blood and a rim of dirt under the nails. Cold, she thought. He feels so cold.

She talked to him, softly, insistently. "It's going to be all right, you're all right, love. I'm right here and everything's going to be all right." She began to croon, repeating that, telling him, again and again, that he would be all right, she would see to it.

Something metal clanged loudly in one of the adjacent curtained areas and Peter's hand stayed loosely open in hers.

After a while a nurse came to walk Hetty out of the unit.

Hetty walked into Peg's arms in the waiting room and stood there with Peg swallowing sobs, telling her, "Go ahead and cry."

In the hours to come, Hetty began to lie to herself. She had to believe the surgeon meant to sound hopeful.

"Anything is possible," she kept repeating to Peter's students and colleagues as they started to come and mill around and sit and wait with her during the long hours between her ten minute visits inside the ICU. Peg had called Hetty's dad, George Gordon, and when George Gordon held out his hands, Hetty let him hold her in his trembling old arms, telling him, "Dad, Daddy, we have to pull Peter through this."

When Peter's friends would look up at her as she came out of the unit she would try to reassure them, even the kids in biker's jackets, the so-called gangsters, and the hulking football players. All seemed to need reassurance. "I'm told that it's going to be an uphill fight," she would tell them. "He might take a long while to heal but Peter has a very strong heart. That's what the surgeon tells me. Peter will be back with us. You'll see. Anything can happen."

It would be a long while before Peg Albright and Hetty would be forced to realize that at least one of the group milling around in that crowded waiting room really did not want to hear that.

5

Day Two

The day after Memorial Day Hetty came downstairs at six-thirty in the morning to find her father on the sofa in the den, his head twisted sideways against the pillows, his long bony, white legs sticking out of his trousers. She opened the drapes and touched his arm. "Dad?" George Gordon sat up and coughed, peering at her. "You ought to see your red eyes," she said. "You've got to have the worst crick in your neck."

She tried not to see him painfully unfolding himself. "Did you take the bread out of the oven last night?" she said, distractedly. "I hope you weren't hungry."

He blinked, confused. "Bread?"

"Never mind," Hetty said. "I didn't hear you come in or I'd have made you come upstairs and sleep in the guest room like a civilized person.

He squinted in a shaft of sunlight. The wattles under his chin jiggled. "Didn't see any bread," he muttered. "I wasn't asleep. Just resting my eyes." He looked hopeful. "You got something in the oven?"

"Oh, for heaven's sake," Hetty said. "No. I just thought...never mind. I really want to get to the hospital."

"Well, I figured I'd come by and drive you over there," he said. His white hair, yellowing at the temples, hung like feathers down his back. He stood up, righted himself, slid his arms into his blazer and leaned over to pinch at the creases sewn into his polyester pants. Hetty felt a familiar twinge of worry at the way he moved, so teetery and off-balance. His shiny-seated trousers hung concave over his bony rear.

As they stepped out of the front door, George Gordon went

into a familiar litany. "Just look at that sky. Anybody misses the sunrise misses the best part of the day." There was a pink line along the horizon. The air smelled of magnolia and the honeysuckle on the back fence. He sniffed appreciatively, blinked at Hetty, looked away and made harrumphing noises as he gazed down the row of streetlights lining both sides. "I hope the police are keeping an eye on this street, Angel," he said. "I heard a lot of motorcyclists up and down. This subdivision isn't what it used to be."

He drove so slowly Hetty had to bite her lips to keep from complaining, but they were still the first ones in the chilly waiting room. The nurses let her go right into the unit.

Peter looked the same. Hetty touched his dry lips with the glycerin swab a nurse gave her. She sat and crooned. Peter stayed absolutely motionless, in some distant silent place.

When she came out of the unit, George Gordon was still in the waiting room, craning his neck and cupping an ear toward the small television set up on a pole in the corner.

"He's much the same," she said. "Peter. Much the same."

Her dad's eyes strayed back to the set.

When Hetty said she might do with a cup of coffee, he got up and went trundling down the hall to the nurses' station. He came back with two Styrofoam cups. There was sugar in the coffee, but Hetty sipped it anyway and sat quietly. Waiting.

George Gordon got to his feet when Peg came in.

"Oh, don't get up," she said. "It's only me. Ten-ton Tessie. Don't even ask how I am. Some days it's hardly worth chewing your foot off to get out of the old trap."

"The old trap?" George Gordon looked confused.

"My house. With my mom in it," Peg said. "To remind me what a lousy housekeeper I am and tell me I've got to do something about my rotten kids. Which I know already."

George Gordon harrumphed again nervously and said he had to be going. He kissed Hetty's cheek. "You sure you don't need anything?"

Peg asked that, too, after George Gordon left.

Hetty didn't want anything.

"I brought the paper," Peg said. "It's wet around the edges." She slid the *Chronicle* out of its sleeve, peeled it open, spread it out, and leafed through it. As she scanned, she asked, absently, "You ever take the bread out of the oven?"

Hetty shrugged. She seemed to be studying the knuckles of her folded hands.

"Those delivery guys make a specialty of tossing these things into the nearest puddle," Peg said, to herself. "They have to make sure to get it good and wet. Another suicide bomber in Israel." She sat up. "We made the *Chronicle*. 'Dobie High Teacher Injured.'"

Hetty looked up.

"On page eighteen," Peg said, showing her. "The A section, but we're way in the back."

The item was in a column, stacked with Memorial Day's "Area Briefs" along with a car-jacking and the disappearance of somebody's six-year-old and an unidentified body in an alley off Montrose.

"Police seek an assailant who struck down Sagemont resident Peter Fenton Bach, 44, in a field near Telephone Road and Beltway Eight after sundown on Memorial Day. The Dobie High School teacher is said to be recuperating at Southeast Memorial hospital."

"Recuperating?" Peg muttered. She flinched, hoping she hadn't said the word aloud, and went on, talking fast, trying to cover it if she had. "I guess we didn't make the home edition. I looked all through my paper at home but I didn't see it, did you?"

Hetty didn't answer. She sat quietly distant, her back straight, her feet crossed at the ankles, slowly crossing and uncrossing her hands.

"You know who that quiet detective looks like, sort of?" Peg said.

Hetty sighed.

"The guy on 'MASH.' Not Hawkeye. The other one. B. J. Honeycutt. The nice quiet one. I think the actor is Mike Farrell."

Hetty closed her eyes.

Peg read the paper.

After Hetty went into the unit for one of her ten-minute visits, several strangers came into the chilly little aqua-tinted waiting room and sat in silence, their faces strained. Peg read and reread the paper and did the crossword. When Johnny Schmulbeck and David Gofor arrived, a little before eleven, she was so glad to see them that she had to fight tears.

Paunchy David came blustering in, shouldering his way through the open door, pink-faced and growly, with Johnny edging along behind, apologetically hunching, trying not to take up too much space in the small room.

"Oh guys," Peg said. "Guys."

Johnny stood looking around. "Hospitals," he said. He made a face. He had that round-shouldered slouch even in high school and, even then, that way of coming all apart every time he lowered himself into a chair. "How're we doin'?" he asked, fearfully eyeing the doorway to the unit.

Peg just looked at him.

"That bad?"

She shrugged. "He's in a coma. He's going to be in a coma. I don't want to talk about it. Hetty will be out in a few minutes and we don't want to be, you know, talking about it." She broke off, looked at Johnny again in an exaggerated double-take. "What's with you?"

"I got a haircut," he said, his dark eyes defensive.

"I'm talking about the green stripes on the shirt and the tie. Where'd you get the tie?"

Johnny shot his cuffs and looked down at himself. "Foley's."

"And your scalp shows," Peg said. "What happened to your hair? Stand up." He unfolded himself to his feet and waited obediently. Peg held him at arm's length. "Where'd you get that shirt? Shees. Pistachio. You got a turtle costume, too?"

"Leave me alone," Johnny said. "My shirt got wet so I stopped and got a new one. It's raining, in case you didn't notice. So I make fun of that bubble on your front? How's Junior doing?"

"Never mind Junior," Peg said. "He's gonna turn into a beach ball but I'll be myself again eventually. I always kind of liked your pony tail. You look like a Marine from the neck up."

"I was a Marine. Once."

"Helluva long time ago," David said.

Johnny's face furrowed into a rueful grin. "You don't approve?"

"Well, I hope you got all the pins out of the shirt," Peg said. "It still has its store-bought creases. Now we know why Hallie doesn't let you pick out your clothes."

"You sound like high school," David said. "Come on."

"He was a doofus then, too," she said. "Look at him blush. Okay, Hallie gave you the anniversary sparkler and that's okay, happy anniversary, but did she pick this out?" She flipped Johnny's tie. "When did you start going in for little white doggies?"

"Read the fine print," Johnny said. "It is, too, me."

The fine print on the tie read, in a continuous diagonal line, "Don't eat the yellow snow."

Peg smiled. "That's more like it."

Dave looked from Peg to Johnny, his teeth glinting in his shiny face. "Johnny's decided to clean up his act," he said. "Even poets clean up once in a while. The girls at the agency think it's great. He looks like an insurance man. Finally."

Johnny looked sheepish. "Dave's been riding me." He glanced around at David. "Leave me alone."

Peg eased herself under Johnny's arm for a hug. "Aw," she said, against his chest, "is this awful or what?" She pulled back then and hugged David long and hard before she pushed away, complaining at the pens in his pocket, waving a hand under her nose. "Aramis. You're drowning out the hospital smell."

Tweedledee and Tweedledum, she thought, both of them terrified for Pete, miserable at being in a hospital, so big and sad a person could hardly stand it.

"Ah, we've all been so lucky, haven't we?" she said. "None of us has ever gotten really sick, even, all these years. Other than to have babies, we haven't had to get near this place. Sure as hell not in this part of it, anyway." She gazed around and lowered her voice. "One of the other patients in there was in a motocycle accident last week. That's his mother and sister, in the corner. And I think the skinny little guy has somebody coming out of a lobotomy or some weird thing. This is one creepy place."

David chewed on his lower lip, nodding at her, uneasily eyeing the entrance to the unit. He puffed out his lips and cast around for a distraction. "Brought you some Krispy Kremes." He gave a sad wheeze. "Been trying to get rid of this gut, but this isn't the moment, right?"

"At least it's cushiony," Peg said.

Dave smoothed his smooth hair. "Have a doughnut. Stick something in your mean mouth." He sat down and leafed through the paper.

"You read about all this at the house?" she asked. "It wasn't in my paper."

"Naw." David cleared his throat. "Johnny came by. But I already knew. My boy, Donny, saw the whole thing. He and the Gilbreath boy and young Chaney, Bill Chaney, just happened to be driving around out there when it happened."

He stared at Peg, sorrowing, and was stilled, briefly. "That son-of-a-bitch really let Pete have it. The kids saw the whole thing. They know who the guy is, too. Some high school kid, one of those bikers. Too stupid to graduate. I imagine the police have picked him up by now. They were looking for him last night. Donny says Peter might have 'dissed' this kid."

"Dished?"

"Disrespected him. At some point. Humiliated him in class. The kid's a gangster." Dave sighed. "Doesn't take much with some of these kids. Donny calls him the Dutchman. Traumatized the hell out of the boys, seeing a thing like that." He gave a sad wheeze. "Donny sat around half the night staring at the tube. He's probably still sitting around over there. I couldn't get him to get dressed this morning."

His nose looked punished. He blew it and mopped at it, shaking his head. "I was just telling Johnny: those kids, now, that's an awful thing, to see a thing like that. It was this biker." He took a bite out of a doughnut.

Johnny broke in. "You know who that is, don't you? You ever hear Pete talk about that kid? One of the ones Pete got to school early to tutor. Kind of a bad situation, I gather. That's what Pete called it. A bad situation."

"I call it a rotten kid," Dave said.

Johnny swallowed. "But it might not be him."

"The Dutchman's a street name, of course," David said. "This kid is Clifford somebody. Van something. Lives in a four-bedroom house over on the corner of Windswept. Bad situation. Place is full of bikers half the time. The boy's been in high school a few years but he can't make it to graduation. Self-anointed. In one of those hokey sects. He's fairly notorious. Made the front page a couple of years ago. Arrested on some kind of a save-your-soul, send-me-money, direct mail ponzi investment scheme."

Johnny rubbed his chin. "I think the old man's in jail somewhere."

David snorted. "The hell you say. The guy's rich. He's in the Netherlands or the South Pacific. Jamaica, maybe." He sighed. "Louise is nuts about Jamaica." He bit into a doughnut, looked down at his front and flipped at a cascade of sugar flakes. "Clifford's daddy is long gone. But the kid is bad news. Born to raise hell."

"I think that's the Hell's Angels," Peg said.

Both men stared at her. "Well," she said, "I think the local bikers are Bandidos. Or Kings. They probably have some Hispanic slogan."

Johnny got up and moved in clumsy shuffles around the room. "The cops have to know all this."

"Oh yeah," David said. "A couple of detectives came by the house last night to see if Donald remembered anything else he hadn't told them."

"Did he?" Johnny asked.

"Well, you know, it was getting dark. But Donald says they ought to check and see if this ring the biker wears might have left some kind of a bruise or cut or something. The biker wears one of those skull rings. Rubies in the eyes. And Donald said he thought he might have been injured. Might have been road rage." He rubbed his chin, so close shaven, Peg thought it looked abraided. "Rotten kid. Pete's knocked himself out for those kids. Hell of a thing. Got my boy sick to his stomach."

Johnny put down the doughnut he'd bitten into. He kept patting at the pocket with his cigarettes in it, and he hunched over, slumped into a corner of the sofa, his legs stretched out in front of him with those enormous boots. Gentle Johnny, too big around for basketball, even back yard basketball, when he was twelve, when Kent Cox and Dave Gofor and Pete used to razz him into trying, poor clown. Too big and far too clumsy, even before the hip replacement. And his lousy daddy all the time poking at him saying, "Try not to hurt anybody, son," with that obnoxious laugh, especially that time he spilled the ice water on those people, trying to make a few bucks as a waiter in San Marcos.

The Field

What summer was that? Peg wondered. Their second summer at Southwest Texas State U., with Johnny's huge dad laughing like a madman when Johnny spilled ice water on the woman. How could anybody pick on a big puppy person like Johnny? He'd just sit there with that sweet, sad, lopsided smile. Not that the old man was any better looking. They both could be Walter Matthau's cousins, with old Walter's rumble-grumble voice and his mouth hanging at half mast half the time. Got to be first cousins. Though there might be a whole congregation of big clumsy guys with blubbery lips and overgrown eyebrows shambling around somewhere in Russia or wherever the Matthau clan started out.

Dave Gofor sure liked those doughnuts. Peg had to smile. He was getting sugar down the front of that expensive suit. Too bad his little newspaper never printed news but all those ads would have to keep bringing in enough for a new Chrysler for Louise every spring.

Johnny had been reading the *Chronicle*. "Things might be better than we thought," he said. "Says here our boy is recuperating."

He was so red-eyed that Peg wilted. "Anything can happen," she said.

They all gazed at Hetty when she came out of the unit, but nobody said anything.

Around lunchtime Dave and Johnny hugged Hetty and Peg again and patted at them and went bumbling off and away.

Three big youngsters with motorcycle helmets under their arms came in after the guys had left. The kids asked Peg if anyone knew anything. When she told them Mr. Bach was in a coma, they sat down, looked at each other, got up and walked out. Peg watched them go, thinking of how all kinds of people, all over town, had to be wondering how Peter Bach was doing. All Pete's students. His fans. Like the big kid in that mall, that Saturday. A big tattooed boy. Came up to Peter and Hetty outside the cinemas, yelling, "Yo there, Mister Bach! You my main man!" Made Hetty smile, but she was used to it. Had to happen all the time. A big kid, Mexican, still yelling as he backed away, telling his friends, possessive, "That's Mister Bach."

After four o'clock a Chinese-American couple, the parents of the youngster somebody said had fallen from a roof, came back into the room. Their surgeon wasn't as considerate as Peter's Indian; you could hear him all over the room every time he talked to those people. Peg and everyone else in that room knew more than they wanted to about the cranium of that boy. The distraught parents came in quietly, sat down on one of the turquoise sofas and waited. The clock on the wall whuffed and the TV purred to itself for a long while before the woman looked up.

"Mister Bach is in there, too?" she asked. Peg nodded. "He's a very good teacher," the woman said. "Very good. You are his wife?" Peg explained that Hetty was Mr. Bach's wife.

The Chinese woman glanced over at Hetty and away, saying, "I am so sorry." After a long silence the tiny woman said, to no one in particular, "Not all teachers good. Mister Cox is not a good teacher."

Her husband frowned at the floor.

"Not good," the Chinese woman went on. "Too big and rough."

The Chinese man's eyes flickered in her direction and the woman bowed her head.

"Kent Cox?" Peg asked.

The woman shook her head, her fingers at her lips.

At four-fifteen a nurse came out and ushered Hetty and the Chinese couple into the unit. After a few minutes the Chinese couple came out wiping their eyes as they walked out of the room and down the hall.

Hetty wouldn't go anywhere after she came out of ICU. She wouldn't even go to the cafeteria.

Peg had to go home to check on the kids.

When she got back, Hetty was right where she'd left her, gazing at her hands folded in her lap, unfocused and pale.

"Got to watch those hands," Peg said, sighing. "Can't let those hands get away from you. Especially the thumbs. You really want to keep track of those thumbs, kid."

Hetty folded her hands under her arms and raised her head.

"It's time you had something to eat," Peg said. "Are you up for a walk to one of those machines in the cafeteria?"

Hetty shook her head.

"Aw, come on," Peg said.

"That doctor might come back," Hetty said. Her voice wavered.

"I'm trying to remember. Some youngster cried, in Peter's classroom, on Friday. He started to mention it but the phone rang and then he was in the shower."

"Ah, don't," Peg said. "I won't cry anymore if you don't." She stook up and rubbed her back. "Don't keep hurting yourself. Look, this whole thing is too crazy to even try to dope out."

Hetty couldn't seem to get her voice under control. "He's so hurt," she said, weeping. "You don't know. His head, that doctor said his head, his brain inside his skull is so swollen. They--"

"It's not *they*," Peg said, yanking at her hair. "It's just one stupid kid. Can you not look like that? Holy hell. We've got to get out of here, Het. For a little while?"

She got to her feet and began pacing, moving heavily perilously close to the edge of a coffee table in the center of the room. "Some dopey kid, on crack or angel dust or whatever. What good does it do to sit around trying to figure it out?"

She sat down again, reached for Hetty's hands and pulled her around so she could see into her face. "We've got to stay sane, here."

Hetty's eyebrows came down into a line beneath pale thumbprint indentations in her forehead. "I'm all right."

"You have to eat," Peg said. "Come on, honey. You're making me crazy. At least walk with me to the cafeteria and try some soup." She sighed. "Dave says his boy won't eat, either. Donald is sitting around staring at the TV with the sound off. Of course, a guy marries a person like lousy Louise, he's got to figure he's gonna have some kind of a kid. Who knows why people marry the people they marry? You've got to wonder about that. There's Dave and Louise with fat Doris and Weird Willie, over there in the palace of dysfunction. How old is Donald? He's got to be one of the weirdest-"

"Peg," Hetty said. "Peg, dear. Talk less. Please."

6

Wednesday. Man. Mr. Bach's got to be hurting like hell this morning, Donald thought. If he's still alive. If he's even awake. Which he probably isn't. Might not ever wake up, slammed up against that truck and his head cracked like an egg. Like in that show where those gangsters stuck that guy's in this vise and turned the handle until he...oh, shit. Mr. Bach.

Donald's mother wondered if he wanted a nice egg and some toast. He didn't want an egg.

His mother said fine and went back upstairs.

He wished both his mom and his dad would leave him alone. Permanently. He had his quilt down on the sofa in the downstairs study and the TV on without the sound turned on so nobody would complain about any noise or anything and now here's his dad, walking around in circles, wanting to know if he slept down here all night.

Like, who slept?

His dad sounded really worried. Donald felt bad about that, sort of, but he had a lot on his mind. What he wanted, mostly, was for his dad to go somewhere and leave him alone.

"Summertime, son," his dad said, loud and cheery. "You want to give young Gilly or Bill a call? See what's up?" He aimed a friendly punch at Donald's bicep but Donald ducked out of the way so he missed and hit the back of the sofa. Sent him off balance for a couple of seconds.

"I pretty well know what's up," Donald said.

"Now, now. Your mother and I know how you feel about what's happened," he said, with this I-mean-it frown. "We're with you all the way, son. Terrible thing. Terrible. Peter Bach is one hell of a guy and we all feel pretty rotten about what's happened. Terrible.

We're in this together."

Yeah, you're a big fan, Donald thought. I've heard you on that. You've got to be the president of Mr. Bach's fan club.

Smells like you've already had your couple of packages of cigarettes. Can't even get a deep breath, can you? Why don't you step out onto the patio and light up another Lucky Strike off of the end of the one you're working on?

His father went clumping off into the kitchen and came back with a cup of coffee, still talking, had to keep talking, puff, puff, puff. "You sick, son? If you're sick, that's one thing. If that's it, you're going to have to let your mother take you over to the clinic so you can be checked out. Either that or get dressed and straighten up, here." He sipped at the coffee and went over and put it down.

Must be too hot, Donald thought. Don't burn your tongue, Dad. That's right. Set it right down on the varnish, there. See if we can't make a nice ring on the table top and make mom hysterical.

His dad shot him a look like he was reading his mind and picked up the coffee, puffed out his lips and stood around rocking from the balls of his feet to the heels, back and forth. "I'm going on over to the hospital, see if there's anything I can do," he said.

"You want me to come along?"

"Dunno if that's such a good idea," his dad said. "Might be better if you think about something else, today. Why don't you give one of your friends a call?"

"Maybe," Donald said. "Dad. You think the cops have picked up the Dutchman?"

"Wouldn't be a bit surprised. I don't think you need to be worrying about that."

"Well, I am," Donald said. "Big time. Why can't I come with you to the hospital?"

"Because that's no place for you to be today, son. I want you to call up somebody, try to get this thing off your mind. You hear me, son?"

Donald heard him.

"I keep thinking about Mister Bach," he said.

"You want me to drive you over to Gilly's?" his dad asked.

"I'm thinking of spending the summer on this sofa," Donald said. "Since I'm never gonna have any wheels."

"Now, now," his dad said.

"Mister Bach was going to show me how to shift," Donald said. "In his Chevy. It's got four on the floor."

His dad looked at his watch. "Yes, well, we can talk about that some other time."

"You gonna do that, Dad? You gonna let me drive the—"

"Now, just a minute, young man."

"No, let's think about that," Donald said, starting to ride his dad because the whole thing about how nobody would let him drive was starting to make him crazy, like it always did. "You gonna buy me a Chevy or a jeep or something because if you're thinking about that maybe we could—"

"You hold on," his dad said, all puffed out. "If Saint Peter was putting all these ideas in your head, we need to—"

"What? Dad? What was that I heard? We calling Mister Bach names today, right now, this morning, that what we're doing?"

"Saint Peter." Donald's dad stared at him, puffing his lips in and out, snapping to how he had fallen in, for a minute there.

"You going to go around calling him 'Saint Pete' some more today?" Donald said. "With him lying in the hospital over there with his head smashed in, dying, that what you're gonna do?"

"That's just about enough of that, young man," his dad said. Total defeat. He had his hands clenched. "You get up off of that sofa and go put your britches on."

Donald almost said, "Go ahead and hit me," but he didn't feel like pushing it any further.

But he took his time getting up and heading for the stairs. "Nothing good on the tube anyway," he said, over his shoulder.

His mom passed him on the stairs and he could hear her and his dad going at it in the kitchen from the landing and all the way up the stairs. Parts of it, anyway, with his mom going, "Did you threaten him? You did. You threatened him, didn't you? Did you stand there and threaten that boy, today of all days?" And his dad going, "You got any ideas? He's all yours, dear." And his mom about half frantic, yelling stuff like sure, fine, what's different and what is she supposed to do anyway? "Am I supposed to pick him up and dress him?" she's yelling, and, "Wouldn't this be a great time for someone to try to be at least somewhat effectual, for a change?"

Man. She loves words like that, Donald thought. "Effectual." His dad is supposed to be somewhat effectual.

"Can you get off that?" His dad's voice dropped out of hearing range.

Poor old Pop, Donald thought.

He slammed his bedroom door and opened it again so he could lean out and listen and really wished he hadn't.

"Your own daughter living in that rabbit warren over there with cockroaches all over the walls and the shower rotted out and teeming with who knows what diseases because she's fed up with trying to live in this house with you," his mother yelled. "Big man. Big man who hits people who can't hit back."

"Aw, Louise," the old man said. "How do you think that makes me feel?"

"Oh, yes, oh, yes, that's right, everything has to be about how you feel, that it?" His mom is beginning to get about half weepy. "Your son is grieving himself to death and we're supposed to be worrying about how you feel. He sees this awful thing and now he's a scared little boy grieving himself sick over the only man who ever really took the time to listen to him, to care if he lives or dies or pay any attention to how he—"

Donald couldn't handle any more. "I'm getting dressed, okay?" he yelled. "I am getting dressed." Damn.

His dad was out of there by the time Donald got downstairs again. His mom was pawing through her attaché case and her purse, fluttering around about being in this "absolute rush, dear" because she had to be over in the west end at some bank in the Galleria in, like, forty-five minutes, for this meeting supposed to be so crucial. All her meetings were always crucial. "I could drop you at the mall or somewhere but you'd have to walk home," she said. "You could do with some exercise. I'm just going to make it," she said, all chirping and chirky. "Where do you suppose Gilly is?"

"Who cares," Donald said.

"This is it," his mom said, looking herself over in the hall mirror, giving her scarf a pat. "Biggest mortgage lender in the Galleria. I get this one lined up and I'm set. We are set."

She tipped her head to get a better look at her mouth. "You

going to be okay?"

"I keep telling you," Donald said. "This guy saw Gilly's car. Gilly's got this recognizable car. And this guy, hell, Mom, I dunno. He goes to Dobie, after all. He knows us. He's probably somewhere around here watching this house right now. Unless they picked him up. You think the cops got him?"

"Well, you can't stay home and cower around," she said, "I don't know about these earrings. The mall has security, if you're so nervous."

"Bill and Gilly said they saw the Dutchman make two of those Almeda Mall renta cops walk backwards for like half the length of Penney's store front, once," Donald said. "You don't have any idea."

She opened her purse and rummaged around in it. "Well, what do you expect me to do?" She started shaking her keys. "How about a movie?"

"How about I ride along to the Galleria?" he said. "I could ice skate." He couldn't believe he'd said that.

Not a bad idea, though. The more he thought about it the better he liked it.

She was fussing with her lipstick, going all around her mouth with this pencil thing. "Oh, I don't think that's such a good idea," she said, when she got through, stretching her mouth in a smile at herself, deciding she might be finished.

"Okay, fine," Donald said, heading back to the living room couch. "Go catch your meeting. I'll be okay." He snapped on the TV, grabbed a pillow and slumped down into the sofa cushions.

"Aw, hell," his mother said. She looked like she was going to cry. "If I get this loan I'll make the million dollar club, Donald. Do you know what that means? Do you realize how hard I've worked for this?" She was so mad she was shaking, her mouth working, just desperate as hell. "All that cold calling. I bought this three-hundred dollar suit and got all dressed up and drove over there and parked my car twice before I could even make myself go in. I just cried. I drove home in tears, Donald. Twice. And now they are waiting for me. I'm in. And all you can do is sit there like a big lump."

She shut up and stood looking at him with tears in her eyes and her chin puckering into a pink peach pit.

"So go," Donald said.

"I give up," she said.

Good.

But he wasn't all that crazy about sitting around by himself all day again, either.

"I could ice skate," he said.

She nibbled at her upper lip, considering, for a minute, while Donald looked around. After a minute she said, "Oh, hell, get in the car. Why not? You can skate. If this goes the way I am praying it will I might even take you over to Rice stadium and let you practice driving, for a little while, on the way home. Provided you quit looking so horrendously wretched." She rumpled his hair.

Forty minutes later they were circling around in the underground garage at the Galleria, looking for a parking space on the third level, when Donald thought he spotted a space and his mother started to pull into it and had to slam on the brakes because the space was taken. There was a Harley in it.

So. Every Harley didn't have to belong to the Dutchman, Donald told himself.

It kind of made his stomach jump and clench, for a couple of seconds there, though.

He looked around at the garage. It had some kind of construction going on. There were all these dim fluorescent bulbs stuck up in a bunch of dark insulation on the ceiling where they were.

Then, the next thing, they got this space and Donald is walking along with his mother with her hurrying, head down, not watching where she's going, pushing past a group of people, sticking her arm up to fend off a couple of women and Donald is thinking boy, she sure can move along in those three inch heels and his mother is almost running when she bumps into the Dutchman.

In front of the Lord and Taylor elevator.

The Dutchman. In a black shirt with *Spirit Untamed* on it, sleeveless so the tattoos on his ropey arms show, the frigate in full sail and the life-sized heart and dagger and the rest, a regular picture gallery of tattoos up and down his shoulders and arms, with the black sweat band around his head, with the pony tail, with the oval shades, shining black. Standing there. Looking at his mom and then, oh, God, at Donald.

He stands there, those dark lenses reflecting, and the Dutchman says, "How you doin'?"

"Okay, I guess," Donald answers, hearing himself squeak. His mom looks the Dutchman over and sort of smiles her smile like at a waiter or somebody and she stands there, staring straight ahead. Waiting for the elevator.

The elevator comes.

They get in. The Dutchman gets in the elevator with Donald and his mother. And he steps over to the key pad and pushes the button for the first floor and says, without looking around, "That do it?"

"Oh, my, no," Donald's mom says, irritated. "We want two." She's running a little late, she explains, and would he mind? But they're already riding past two. Nobody says anything for a minute because by then even his mom is catching on that this is not somebody she really wants to be riding around with in this little box for any length of time and she says, of all things, in this ridiculous voice, "Well, it'll only be a minute or so, I suppose."

The Dutchman turns to face Donald. Donald can smell this leather smell and see part of his face, his eyes, mostly, shining in the black ovals. His mom grabs his hand and gives him a little yank back but she doesn't make a sound, Thank You, God. They stand there staring at the wall with nobody making a sound until they get to the first floor and the Dutchman gets off the damned elevator and walks away.

"Good heavens," old Mom goes, as soon as the door closes and they're by themselves. "Lord and Taylor isn't what it used to be."

Donald can't say anything. His mouth is too dry. As soon as he can get some spit so his tongue will work he says, fast, "That's him. That's the guy. The Dutchman. That's the guy slugged Mister Bach. That's him. He's the one."

"The man you told the police about?" His mother looks around uneasily and a little bit scared but mostly confused. Then she turns on him, about half irritated, with about eighty-seven emotions working around on her face until irritation takes over. "If you told the police all about him well, then, you'd think they would be keeping track of this, this person. If he's so dangerous what's he doing out shopping? I mean, wouldn't they have arrested him if he's the one? How can he be the one? Look around. We're in Lord and Taylor's, for goodness sake. You don't have to go all sweaty and weird on me, Donald."

"Mom," Donald says, "Mother, listen to me. That's the guy. I swear to God."

"Well," his mother says. "What's he going to do, beat you over the head with a shopping bag with a big rose printed on it?"

She fumbled around in her purse and handed Donald a couple of twenties with a big toothy smile, like end of discussion. "We can talk about all these things all the way home," she said. "After you have your little driving session. Now, go ice skate. Try to forget about all these awful things. Enjoy yourself a little, can't you?"

Enjoy himself.

Donald couldn't believe it.

Then he could.

"Go," he said. "Have a nice meeting." And he walked away, fast, wishing he had a Kleenex because he was so mad it was making his nose run and there were these clerks looking at him, not paying much attention, but still. When he walked past one of the clerks she handed him a little piece of cardboard with some kind of perfume on it and he thanked her but he damned near walked right into a mirror trying to get out of there.

When he got to the store's mall entrance his mom almost caught up to him. She waved a little wave, saying something about meeting him at the rink where they always met, at the skate rental, as soon as she could break loose and couldn't he at least wish her luck, honey, while he was looking around, wondering whether somebody is reflected in the edge of one of the mirrors behind her.

And there he is.

He is standing over near the top of an escalator, looking around like he owns the store and everything in it.

Just standing there. Watching.

Donald turns and goes tearing back into the store the other way. He's on the escalators on the other side, the going down one, when he looks back and he doesn't see any big dark guys behind him but a couple of minutes after he starts walking around on the next floor and he has to sort of touch a wall to keep his knees from buckling because there he is, again, the Dutchman, reflected in a mirrored wall, standing there, with those black shades turned his way. With this kind of a pulled back look to his mouth that doesn't look anything like any kind of a smile.

Donald shoved some people around getting onto an up escalator so he could get away from there and hurry out and run down a hall, past a bookstore and a bunch of plants.

Only there wasn't much of anywhere to go, then, except to the tower elevators right there in front of him or back onto another escalator or on around the corner with a crowd of people with some little kids clamoring to go into the Disney store. Donald sidled over and walked along with the chattering little crowd headed into the Disney store, trying not to look back until he realized the people around him were all Japanese and about a foot shorter than he was, nobody in the bunch even coming up as high as his chest—

—and there he is, the Dutchman, sauntering along back there, coming right on into the Disney store, what in the hell is he doing coming into the Disney store? Strolling in, punching his fist into his palm, with these black oval mirrors turned Donald's way.

As Donald turned around a goofy, forlorn, little voice in his head started in sing-songing a kind of a halfway hysterical refrain of a nursery rhyme ditty that Doris used to sing at him sometimes when she got stuck baby-sitting him when he was a little kid and was mad at him, that got both of them in trouble because it used to scare Donald so bad that he'd wet the bed because he'd be too scared to get up and go to the toilet. "Fee, fi, foh, fum," the little voice whimpered, in the back of his head. "Fee, fi, foh, fum. I smell the blood of an Englishman. Be he alive or be he dead, I'll break his bones to make my bread" as Donald walked out of the store fast, telling himself to get a grip; trying not to giggle. Because if he started giggling he might not be able to quit giggling.

And that might be a real bad idea. Because he had a strong feeling he might need some oxygen real fast any minute now to get his legs moving.

7

The Dutchman

Walk, Donald tells himself. Now. Fast.

But he can't. He has to get past all these jabbering little kids, a whole mess of rugrats that he damned near trips over, with their mother—or whoever—hollering at him. All excited about the situation. But what is she doing letting these little kids futz around with these plastic dinosaur things clicking around all the hell over the floor?

By the time he gets to the door of the store he has the breathing thing under control and the legs working. Donald lifts up his knees and runs.

He runs down a down escalator. Runs alongside the ice skating rink, the length of the rink. Stands panting in front of some kind of a luggage store with these tourists in front of it, staring at him like they think he's some kind of a freak so he pulls up and stands around looking for some place to duck out of sight.

A jewelry store has this narrow space between a couple of panels but while he's looking at them, wondering whether a person could slide in there, this officer, a woman in a gray and black security uniform, comes walking up. Does he need any help?

Yeah, Donald thinks, he sure does. But he thanks her and walks alongside her trying to make conversation, asking her about this badge she's got on, how long has she had it and how hard was it to get her job and did any of the security guys have any guns or anything. After a couple of minutes of that the security woman starts to look kind of irritated and Donald starts to get halfway ashamed of himself. She doesn't even come up to his chin for crying out loud, she's this little short woman with a gray streak in her hair.

"I'm pretty racked up about this guy," he starts to tell her but that sounds so weird he gives up on it and sort of switches over to would she please tell him how to get to the men's room.

He gets all the way to the end down by the post office before he looks back to see if she might still be standing there, looking at him like a person didn't have any right to walk around in a mall.

He looks all around. No Dutchman.

What he has to do is sit down and think.

There are these seats for people to sit on while they put on their skates for the ice rink but there aren't but about a couple dozen people sitting around right now.

The Zamboni rides back and forth, smoothing the ice. Donald sits watching it, looking up and around the upper levels. He keeps wishing he could find some kind of a crowd to maybe blend in with. He goes over to the rail of the rink and looks up at the faces looking down from the other levels and gets spooked. The damned ice rink is like a stage.

He stands up and sits down again, telling himself to knock it off. Far as he can see everything's okay. There's this mannequin next to a sunglasses kiosk with the black sunglasses on. Donald sits there looking at that thing, thinking, boy, those shades look just like the Ray Bans that the—

—and the mannequin takes a step.

In his direction. With those black lenses glinting back and forth and finally, God, at him.

Donald gets up and runs.

He doesn't look behind him until he gets halfway around the second level when he does let himself look. He doesn't see the Dutchman anywhere. He ducks into this narrow little shop with a rental tuxedo in the window.

Not a very big shop. Empty. Only has one clerk in the place.

"Okay if I use the john?" Donald asks, trying to get some air in his lungs as he trots past the clerk.

The clerk looks up from polishing the shelf in a counter and said, "Sorry, man. No rest room here. You got to use the public rest room."

Donald keeps on going to the back of the store.

The clerk straightens up, shaking his head, talking some more

The Field

about some public rest rooms down the hall and across the way somewhere.

"Yeah, well, I got an emergency," Donald says.

"Hey, man, I'm sorry," the clerk says but by then Donald has reached this door marked "Employees Only."

"Hey, dude," the clerk says, hustling up behind him, "you can't go in here. This is my first day and you're gonna get me fired. No toilet here."

But he's wrong. There is this "Employees Only" door and behind it there is this room with a washbasin and sure enough, a stall with a door with a toilet behind it. Donald gets in the stall, hooks the door shut and tells the clerk to chill out. "Hey, I won't tell anybody if you don't," he says, and he starts practically begging the man to go on back and polish his counter or whatever and leave him alone.

Has to be pretty stupid. Donald knows that. Like, how long will he be able to stay in here? But at least he's out of sight for a couple of minutes and he's got to have some time to think, is all.

Maybe the crazy Dutchman will get bored or have to go meet somebody. Maybe he has some reason for hanging around the damn Galleria and he'll go do it, whatever it is, and get back on his Harley and get out of there.

But the clerk is all excited, so Donald is thinking what the hell, bad move—

—when he hears the Dutchman say, out in the store, "How you doin'?" and a kind of Mickey Mouse noise that had to be the clerk, answering.

So Donald climbs up and crouches on the toilet so his shoes won't show under the door.

Then he decides that's even more stupid but he can't move. He can't make his legs work. All he can do is hunker in there like an idiot moron, crouched up on this crazy toilet lid, hugging his knees, when he hears the door open and then he is staring through the open crack along the edge of the stall door—

—at those shades.

Because there he is, the Dutchman, leaning on the wall out there like he doesn't think Donald is all that interesting but he hasn't got anything better to do.

After a couple of long breaths, Donald hears himself whisper, "Hi, there."

The Dutchman grunts. "You got a prob?"

Donald can't imagine what in the hell the man is saying.

Then he can.

"Problem?" Donald gets his legs under control and slides his feet to the floor and straightens up. He inhales. "Nope." He unhooks the latch and opens the door and eases out, thinking, Now I am going to get my head held in a toilet. But the Dutchman just stands there with his head kind of back and to one side, like he's kind of pondering.

After a couple of minutes he takes off the shades and stands looking at Donald with these eyes, oh, man, the eyes worse than the black shades, light gray eyes, gun metal, with these little points of light, under the shaggy black brows.

One of the eyebrows lifts. "Whassup?"

"Yeah, well." Donald swallows. "Not much."

Donald starts in explaining. "I got this stomach problem," he whispers. "I'm, like, sick. Sort of."

That gets him a long look and he nods. Stands there and nods. Like some kind of a yo-yo.

After a couple of minutes Donald swallows some more and nods some more and when he quits nodding the Dutchman is still standing there kind of cleaning his teeth with his tongue, bored, not moving and not letting Donald move. Not letting Donald out of that stall.

He shrugs those tattooed shoulders and yawns and turns around and strolls over and opens the door to the store and he is going away, oh, Thank You, God, the Dutchman is going on out of there—
—but he stops and turns around. "How's Mr. Bach doin'?"

"Not so hot, I guess," Donald says.

"Not gonna make it," the Dutchman says. He bows his head. "Somebody gonna pay for that." He's got this growl. "Somebody pays."

His eyes are slate gray. Like gray ice. "You get the numbers on that plate?"

It takes a minute before Donald knows what he's saying. "On the t-t-truck?" he asks. "The license numbers?"

The Field

The Dutchman looks at him.

"Ask a stupid question," Donald babbles. "It was a Ford. Four something and maybe an 'M' on it, I'm pretty sure of the 'M'. With an 'E' and a 'Q', maybe." He swallows. "I oughta know a Ford, man. My dad had a Ford pickup we used to keep up at the lake. He used to all the time be mad at it. He would all the time go: 'Ford', like, 'fix or repair daily' because it all the time broke down but my dad doesn't take care of cars much, he's kind of—"

The Dutchman's got his hand up. "What did he do with it?"

"My dad?"

The Dutchman looks at him.

"The Ford, you mean? Our pickup?"

The Dutchman's mouth kind of tucks in at the corners. Donald really wishes he wouldn't do that.

"The truck?" Donald asks. "Yeah. Well, it kind of died. I worked on it some but it died, you know. Then we donated it to Mr. Cox's class at Dobie. The kids in Automotive worked on it and got it running. Mr. Cox drove that thing for a while. The Cocksman. I don't know what he finally did with it. Geez. You think that could be the truck?" He slaps his brow. "I bet it could be. How come I didn't snap to that?"

He has to slap his brow again, trying to quit running his words together. "I bet that was it. I shoulda recognized it but I dunno. I don't think it was. But that's what my dad finally did with our truck. Gave it to the Cocksman. He's got a Toyota now, though. The Cocksman."

The Dutchman puts his hand up, again. Donald shuts up and swallows.

"Think you saw Cox?"

"Oh, geez. Mr. Cox? Oh, man," Donald echoes. "I don't know. I don't know. I don't think but it might have been. Might have been anybody, you know? In the dark, out there? I told the lieutenant about our truck. But that wasn't the license on our truck or anything so I don't think—"

"Don't," the Dutchman says, staring hard. "Don't. Think. You talk too much."

"I know it," Donald says.

"Don't think," the Dutchman goes. "With cops, you don't *think*.

You be sure." He raps Donald on the chest with the back of his hand. "Got that?"

He puts on his shades and turns away. "We were in San Antonio," he says. "Memorial Day."

"San Antone," Donald says. He tries for a quiet rebel yell. "Eeehaw." It comes out in a croak.

"Tell Miz Bach we're on it," the Dutchman goes.

He walks out into the store. Donald hears him say, "How ya doin'?" to the clerk. He peeks out in time to see the clerk duck down behind a counter.

Right then, standing in the back of that store with the Dutchman walking out of there and the clerk peeking around the counter mopping at his face with a towel, begging Donald to kindly get the hell out of there, please, with Donald swallowing like a mad man, trying to get rid of this coppery taste on his tongue—

—right then, something comes to Donald.

It's so obvious that he has to smack himself on the forehead again because even he should have known it right off the bat. That couldn't have been the Dutchman out in that field. Not just because the Dutchman wouldn't be caught dead in any crummy pickup truck when he's got this Harley costs like about twenty or thirty or forty thousand bucks. And not just because he said he was in San Antonio with the Bandidos who would all lie like rugs if the Dutchman said. But because the Dutchman has God only knows how many guys to slap somebody around if he wants somebody slugged. All he'd have to do would be give somebody the nod. Period.

And the reason he kept following Donald all over the crazy Galleria had to be to find out what Donald and Gilly and Bill saw, on Memorial Day.

And how Mr. Bach is doing.

That has to be it. And now he's *on* it. He and the whole, crazy, easy ridin', Bandido gang. *On* it.

Oh, man.

Donald walks out of the store and over to the railing of the ice skating rink and grabs that rail to lean on, his insides going hot and cold with relief, boy, he all of a sudden realizes he really needed to get to the men's room.

Donald is looking around trying to remember what that clerk

in the tux rental place said about how to get to the nearest men's room when he glances into this store with nothing in the window but this one black and white mannequin in some kind of a man's silk suit, with this brass plate that says "Emporio/Armani" up on this marble panel over to the side in front.

And the Dutchman walks in there. Into that shop.

Unbelievable.

So maybe he came to the Galleria to get a tuxedo or whatever.

Donald walks *away* and keeps on keeping on, one foot in front of the other, walking until he can run, so he can make it to the men's room. Just in time.

8

On Thursday morning Peg came into the waiting room in a new linen maternity jumper with her pale hair tucked into a silver barrette and her eyes puffy little red exes. "Had a fairly strenuous difference of opinion about the boys with mom, last night," she told Hetty. "I'm not quite sure what happened. One minute I'm thanking mom for the jumper and the next thing she's saying I can probably wear it after the baby is here since I'm obviously going to be so 'terribly outsized' and that segued into the kids' table manners and Jerome's rotten character—right in front of the boys—and then I guess I said some things I'm gonna regret." She grimaced. "Gonna, hell. So how's by you? Did you sleep at all?"

Hetty said she'd slept.

"Liar, liar, pants on fire," Peg said. "You didn't either. Look at you."

Hetty thanked her.

"You're welcome," Peg said. "And now look who's coming up the hall. How do we get so lucky? You talk about farting in silk."

"Peg," Hetty said. She winced, hoping Louise Gofor hadn't heard.

Evidently she hadn't. Louise had on white silk slacks with a dry cleaner's crease and a silk blouse with a sheer scarf in a large soft bow at the side of her long neck.

"Oh, sweetie," she said, kissing Hetty, "how are you, really and truly?" She didn't wait for an answer.

"This is all so ghastly," Louise went on, her hands smoothing at her hair. "I tried all day yesterday to get over here but at least Dave was here with you, wasn't he? And somebody has to pay attention to Donny. Donny is taking all this so hard. He loves Peter and you so. We all do. But you know that."

She hugged Peg, said, "kiss-kiss," glanced around the room and added, lowering her voice, "I hope the guys are some comfort. Johnny and Dave can get on a person's nerves."

Every time she tucked her hair behind her ear she glanced at the ceiling. "I get so fed up with David's being such a soft touch. But I guess Johnny and Hallie can't help being so, you know."

"Do I know?" Peg asked.

"Yes," Louise said. "Of course you do. Needy. No. Needful. So needful."

"Ah," Peg said.

Louise held Peg at arm's length, appraising her. "You mustn't put on too much weight, dear."

Peg's teeth flashed in a brilliant wide grin. "Weight?" she asked. "I haven't noticed any increase in gravity." She glanced around. "You notice any increase in the gravity around here?"

Louise appeared vaguely mystified. "Well. It's not all that healthy," she murmured. "All that weight."

"Keeps a person from bumping around on the ceiling," Peg said. Her voice went sweet. "Though some people think it's not gravity at all. Just that the earth sucks. Speaking of weight, how's Doris doing?"

Louise stiffened. "My daughter happens to have a glandular problem."

"And one of my sons is dyslexic," Peg said, "Tough world, isn't it, kid?"

"Peg," Hetty said.

Peg looked contrite. "Oh, don't mind me," she said.

"I never do," Louise said. She untied and retied her scarf. "Actually, I'm only here for a minute, loves. I've got an appointment." She perched on a chair. Her mouth pursed. "You'd think those nurses would do something about this crowd. Some of these people look, you know. Downright germy."

Peg's smile showed her back teeth. "Germy?"

"You know what I mean," Louise said. "Look at those tattoos."

"Oh, those," Peg said. "It's common knowledge about tattoos. Hot beds of germs. They're probably spraying germs all over the place like little lawn sprinklers."

Louise glanced at the ceiling. "Well, I just mean, you'd think the nurses would say something."

"They do," Peg said. "Every once in a while. They keep trying. I think that one in the doorway is staring this way. You have any tattoos?"

"You all are going to have to find some other place to wait," the nurse announced.

"See?" Peg said.

"Oh, you're so funny," Louise said, but she got up, gathered her purse and attaché case and said her farewells.

The nurse wasn't as successful at shooing away the rest of the crowd. By two o'clock, when Johnny and David came in, people were lining up along the walls of the corridor again. So many people seemed to make David uneasy. There was no place to sit. He stood around jingling the change in his pockets and fiddling with his keys, on a key ring with what looked like a big, fat, glittering diamond on it.

"Where'd you get the key ring?" Peg asked.

"When we went to the diamond mine, in East Texas," he said. "Months ago."

"Blinding," Peg said.

"You know you love it," he said, absently. "Next time we go, I'll get you one." He tucked the key ring in his pocket and looked around. "Getting almost hard to breathe in here. You know any of these folks? I know some of the teachers. The tattooed guys have to be students. Or alumni, God save us."

"Hetty belongs to these organizations," Peg explained. "And they belong to her. Boy, do they. That man with the orange hair and the green eye shadow? Has to be Art League. I think he's famous. Does murals. And the kid next to him with the stud in his tongue? Probably one of the teachers. That bunch in the corner might be whatchamacallits. Water colorists. They can be really strange. The tall guy in the shirt that says 'WASH' is the president, I think. He broke down, a little while ago. That's what all that patting and fussing is about. Doesn't he make you think of Clint Eastwood?"

"No," David said. He glanced around. "Louise and I met some of the watercolorists. They came by Hetty's last night. Louise happened to see them pull up over there so she ran across the street. Don't know which outfit they belong to. Called themselves whivvers. I sneaked away upstairs to play on the computer and left Louise stuck with them. She said she tried to make conversation but she had to toss in the towel. 'Those women don't know anything about bridge and golf or real estate or anything,' she says. 'One of them never heard of the Astros or Minute Maid Park.' They brought food for Hetty, though. Our freezer is filling up. Hetty's gonna have a life time supply of Stouffer's."

"WIVLA," Peg said, after a minute.

David looked blank.

"That's who that is." Peg said.

"That right?" David wheezed.

Peg nodded. "The Women in the Visual and Literary Arts. WIVLA. Hetty's on the board, or she used to be. They have these big shows and stuff. Like at the Jung Center? And the Bank of America, downtown? Those paintings with the poetry and like that? That's WIVLA. I think Hetty's got paintings in both those shows."

"That right?" David tilted his head. "There's that lieutenant. What's his name. Gray. Talking to the bikers. Looks like they're leaving."

"Good," Johnny said. "I was beginning to think they were settling in until closing time."

The bikers left but Johnny and George Gordon stayed all afternoon and evening until a nurse came out of the unit to kick everybody out. All the way to the car, George Gordon fussed and sputtered, worrying about the motorcyclists in the parking lot, insisting Hetty should come stay at his house.

Hetty didn't want any part of that. She didn't want to go home with Peg, either. "I want to go home to Shadow, in my own house, with my own bed in it," she insisted.

She didn't realize how tired she was until she'd gotten into the house. She kept leaning against things, thinking she really ought to eat, but the thought of food made her queasy. The kitchen smelled stale and faintly yeasty. She broke off a part of a loaf of bread on a towel next to the sink. It hadn't fully baked. The pans must have scorched the cup towel under them. She thumped the loaves into the trash, along with the scorched towel, bagged the trash up and took it out to the can in the garage, wondering if it was Louise Gofor who had come over and taken that bread out of the oven for her. Or Donny, maybe.

*

On Friday morning, Hetty drove herself to the hospital in muggy predawn dark. Fifty percent chance of showers, according to the radio. "Some showers might be heavy," the car radio warned. "Remember Allison, last Spring. Avoid all flooded underpasses. We're getting into the tropical storm season."

She listened, thinking dully that there might not be so many people in the waiting room if the weather turned really nasty and the streets started flooding again. Johnny and Hallie Schmulbeck's house had water right up on the front porch during Allison. That would have to be the last straw for Hallie, to have that house get flooded. Johnny had such a hard time getting his timid little wife out of the house. Louise said she couldn't get past the front door without quaking.

Johnny worries about her so, Hetty thought. I really mustn't let him spend so much time in that waiting room. He can't afford to sit around so much. David always has time on his hands. All he's missing is his golf and it's raining anyway. But Johnny really ought to be concentrating on selling insurance. I'll see if I can't send him on his way, today, when he comes by. Gentle Johnny. Suffering so.

Thinking of the misery in his eyes made her eyes sting.

She was far too early. The nurses might be annoyed. They surely wouldn't let her into the unit. The hospital corridors had an eerie, hollow, predawn feel. Hetty walked throgh the empty waiting room and peeked through the door into the unit. The door was, surprisingly, standing slightly ajar.

And someone, a man, was in there, standing next to Peter's bed. He had on a black pullover and sweat pants and was far too big to be the little Indian doctor.

Hetty stood quietly, wondering, briefly, which of the doctors might have come by in such an early morning costume. The man next to the bed looked as if he might have been jogging and stopped by to—

—to lean over Peter.

When he straightened up Hetty straightened too, and stared. "What are you doing in there?" she asked and had to ask it again, because her early morning voice came out sounding croaky.

One of the nurses at the nursing station in the unit heard her and turned around. She called out, flustered. "Sir? Are you supposed to be in here?" Then, beginning to be angry, she stood up and moved hastily to the side of Peter's bed. "What do you think you're doing? Sir?"

9

The Unit

The nurse's voice went shrill. "I'm calling security. You'll have to leave. At once."

Hetty's heart started to squeeze and pound as the nurse gave the man a shove and he came toward the door of the unit. She couldn't seem to get her feet to move so she could get out of the way as Kent Cox came toward her in a hasty stumble, his shoulders lifted almost to his long ears in an exaggerated shrug, saying, "Aw," as he began to explain.

Babble babble, Hetty thought, why are you babbling?
Kent caught her up in a bear hug and wouldn't let go until she pushed at him. He smelled faintly of Milo and some strong soap and Old Spice.

"Couldn't sleep," he said. "Just kept going over all this and thinking about you, gosh, about how you're taking this, you get any sleep? You probably aren't getting any sleep, either, that's the thing, thing is I got so fed up with sitting around useless. I got dressed and got over here and everything looked pretty quiet in there and I figured what the hell, I could go on in and talk to the man, Peg says that's what you do, sit there and talk to him." He held up a hand to keep her from saying anything as he drew in a hasty breath. "Didn't you say the doctor said to, ah, you know, talk to him and pray and like that?"

He had beads of perspiration on his balding brow and dark mushrooms puffed out beneath his eyes. His uneven breaths were beginning to break into nervous sobs.

Hetty drew away, sat down and patted the seat beside her on the aqua vinyl sofa. "It's all right," she said. "As soon as he wakes up, this will all be over with."

The Field

Kent's eyes pulled down. "You think?" He looked even less assured when a security man hurried in, heard him out and stood around looking annoyed and slightly confused, jingling some keys and a telephone. "Only family supposed to be allowed inside Intensive Care," the man said, interrupting Kent's abject apologies.

When Hetty explained that he was only a "somewhat impetuous friend" the man in his jingling uniform hustled in to confer with the nurses. He came out saying he had to get back up to the roof.

As soon as the security man left Kent said he had chores to do but he'd be back. He went off to the cafeteria and came back with a tuna sandwich for Hetty before he took off.

Hetty had one visit inside the unit before David Gofor came into the waiting room around eleven with Johnny Schmulbeck in tow.

By the time Peg got there the waiting room was beginning to be so crowded that Peg made a big thing of using her elbows to get past Johnny and Dave to give Hetty a hug. She was in a new maternity dress, pink, with a crisp white collar. "Mom went by Dillard's," she said, looking down at herself. "What do you think? Am I a pink elephant or what?"

"You're a pushy broad," Johnny said. "But we're used to it."

Peg made a derisive noise. "If you lived with my mom, you'd catch on. She's got the boys shopping. Trying on clothes. I'm serious. I remember shopping with my mom when I was a kid. 'Stand up straight.' She used to yank my hair. The boys might be scarred for life but you gotta hand it to her. My mother has character." She looked at Hetty. "You eat anything?" Hetty didn't seem to hear.

"Right," Peg said. She looked at the men and groaned. "Looks like business is booming. I'm not the only one all dressed up. The suit doesn't quite hide the belly, Dave, but you get points for a classy try. At least Jerome hasn't got those broken veins across his nose. He called me up last night. Wanted to know about all this. Like he cares. And look who's here."

Kent Cox was back. He ducked down and wrapped Hetty in his long arms. "Milo's in the car," he said. "Can't stay too long." He looked even more rumpled and furry than usual, pounding Johnny's shoulder, shaking David's hand. He stood around with his big round face as sorrowing as Johnny's and Dave's, saying, "You believe this? You believe this?" asking about Johnny's Emily and Dave's Doris and young Donald.

"Ah, don't ask," David said, with a sad snort. "Doris is still droning along dispatching. My daughter the police dispatcher. And I don't know about Donald. Kid's a lost soul. Johnny's girl, Emily, is going to go off to San Marcos to Sweet Sue on a scholarship. No danger of that with either of my kids." He looked over at Johnny and his voice dropped. "Don't ask Johnny about Emily. Empty nest. You know."

"I went by the house," Kent said. "Should have known you wouldn't be there. Left you a frozen lasagna, Hetty. Stuck it in the freezer. Stouffer's. They're pretty good. Not as good as yours."

The men sat down, gazed at the floor and sat around making small miserable noises until Peg thought, oh, why don't they just go away? David smoothed at his pale, graying hair, pinched at his pink nose and made ruminating noises. Johnny tugged at his hairy eyebrows. Kent kept looking at Peg and gazing in Hetty's direction and looking away, swallowing. The noise level kept going up in the small room.

"Got to get my girl out of that dead-end job," Dave said, over the conversations around him. When no one seemed interested enough to comment, he laughed his nervous little laugh and tried to suck it back in. "I was just thinking. Pete helped her get that job. Guess he thought it might be a good idea." He stood up and sighed. "Louise tells everybody Doris is in real estate." He sighed again. "Might be time I sauntered by the paper for a spell."

All three men seemed to think that was a good exit line.

Pete looked worse, greenish, during the afternoon and six o'clock visits. Hetty tried to tell herself that sunken look might mean that some of the swelling was going down.

When she came back out to the waiting room, the crowd seemed to fall silent for what felt like several long moments. Faces turned toward her and turned away. A youngster, one of the bikers, sidled up to murmur something about how he'd turned off an oven. Hetty thanked him. He said something else she didn't quite catch. Something about how sorry he was, how he was going to help her and help some one else, did she understand? No, Hetty thought. I don't.

The Field

I don't want to try to understand...anything. He looked so sweaty and earnest that she thanked him, got up, and walked away, walked out of the room and kept walking down the hall. She could hear people begin chattering again behind her, filling the little waiting room with sound.

She trudged all around the hospital watching rain spatter against windows, saying pieces of prayers inside her head, even though she knew that was crazy, even though she never could believe in a deity like some kind of a bellhop who could be called on to fix a broken brain on a whim just because somebody asked Him to, what kind of a god would monkey around with natural laws like that? Peg had once insisted that that kind of a god must have Alzheimer's, in today's world. Or maybe what she said was that it was that kind of a god created Alzheimer's. But Hetty told herself that maybe, just this one time, for this one person, it wouldn't be so very wrong to ask the creator of the universe to step up, please, front and center, suspend a few of his laws, here, for a little while and fix Pete, please, help Pete, God—

—and along came Peg, looking for her, marching flat-footed up the hall in her big, pink, starchy dress, her eyes narrowing in sad creases at catching Hetty with her brow against a cool window pane. Peg started in wanting her to go downstairs to that awful cafeteria or eat a sandwich wrapped in plastic out of a machine.

When Hetty said she didn't want a sandwich, Peg got in front of her and stood blowing and puffing and moving her head from side to side.

"Go on home and rescue the kids from Leona," Hetty said. "I'll be okay, Peg. Truly."

"You won't, either," Peg said, her face going blotchy. She leaned against the wall with her arms folded. "I'm not going anywhere until you come with me. There's no damned point in your hanging around here for hours and hours when you only get to go into that crazy unit for those spaced-out ten minute visits. Can't you see how crazy-making that is?"

Yes, Hetty told her, she knew. But why couldn't she go on home to her children and leave her alone for a bit?

All of a sudden Peg's lips blew in and out and she was snorting and sobbing. "Well, damn it, I can't stand this and you can't either," she blubbered. "You're hooked up to somebody on life support and all those tubes are tightening and tightening and they're strangling you, too, I'm sorry, but you know it's true." She ran out of breath but she couldn't seem to stop and she would not move out of the way.

Hetty put her brow back against the cool window. "I'm where I have to be."

"In a pig's eye," Peg said, crying harder. "What's there to watch in this place? There's nothing. Nothing."

"People," Hetty said. She didn't know why she said that. Then she did, in a foggy sort of way. "I have to watch."

"Watch? "Peg's eyes narrowed. "What the hell does that mean?"

"I don't know." Hetty closed her eyes. "I don't know."

"No, oh no," Peg said. She quit being so noisy. Her voice dropped almost to a whisper. "Are you trying to figure out who? Who it could have been? Because you cannot do that. You can't look around at us and start thinking that way. Hell, honey. Everybody, we're all hurting. Kent and Johnny and Dave are just—we're all hurting with you. Hell, I even saw Jerome sitting in his truck out in the parking lot, just now, who could believe it? God," Peg whispered. "You've got to get out of here, at least for a breather. You've got to stay sane, honey. This might take a long while."

"Go home, Peg."

"It's not home, any more," Peg said, tears running down her cheeks and chin. "I don't know what I'm going to do about you, you're all I have now and I love you so much and now you're going crazy and I don't know how I'm going to make the house payments or what I'm going to do about the kids my mother thinks they're the worst kids in the world and they're not, they're not, they're just dying all over the place too." Her voice broke and she started crying, again, "And now you're getting sick on me. Don't go nuts on me, can you not?"

"Okay." Hetty said. She swallowed. "But we're losing him," she whispered. "Oh, Peg. My life. My whole life."

Peg grabbed her. They hugged each other and swayed, weeping together.

*

On Saturday a lot of the faculty of Dobie high school joined the

The Field

crowd in the waiting room. People stood along the hall outside the unit and some, the younger ones, sat on the floor. Peg saw the Gilbreath boy, Gilly, and singled him out, tugged on his shirt sleeve and made him come with her for a walk down the hall. "I'm told you got to that field right after Mr. Bach's attack," she said to the kid. "What did you see?"

Gilly told her what he'd told the cops and his mom and the neighbors and all the kids who kept calling him up, asking about that night.

Peg listened. Then she asked the same question Gilly's mom asked. "What were you doing out on Telephone Road?"

"Cruising," the boy said. He couldn't meet her eyes.

"That's a pretty rough area," Peg said.

"Yes, ma'am." The boy squirmed. "I got to get back to my buddies."

"All kinds of stuff going on over there," Peg said. "Dope peddling. Ladies of the night. All kinds of trouble. Nothing but trouble."

"Yes, ma'am."

Peg stood and looked at him, thinking he had to be too young for ladies of the night. "Does your mom know you were out there?"

"Yes, ma'am," the boy said. "Those detectives came to our house." He squared his shoulders. "They've talked to us a bunch of times. Me and Donald Gofor and Bill Chaney."

"But I am told the detectives think you came up with the wrong man," Peg said.

"Yeah," Gilly said. "Maybe." He looked around. "Don figures they're right. That it couldn't of been the Dutchman. Because he was supposed to be on this ride, in San Antonio, and I guess that's what Lieutenant Gray thinks, but me, I dunno. Alls I know is, the guy sure looked like the Dutchman. Had a lot of hair, sort of like Mister Cox's, only in a pony tail. Sure wished I had my cell phone along, but I didn't." He flushed. "Well, my mom has one I usually carry."

"So all you're sure of is that he was a big dark-haired man?" Peg asked.

Gilly nodded. "Only we couldn't honestly tell how dark his hair was." He hesitated. "Funny how you remember stuff but you don't, you know? It's kind of spotty. Most of the guys waiting around up here are pretty big."

"That they are," Peg said "Johnny and Dave used to be tall and skinny, but you couldn't tell it by looking at David now. They played basketball all the way through Southwest Texas. And Kent was a fourteen-pound baby."

"That so?"

The boy didn't look particularly interested in Kent Cox's birth weight. Peg had to smile at herself in some confusion. She couldn't remember how she came by that bit of trivia. "We all know all about each other, I guess," she said, airily, "Have, for years and years. It's important to keep your same old friends." That came out sounding pretty lame and preachy but the boy nodded, with a solemn frown. "Mister Cox explained to the cops about the truck," he said.

Peg snapped into focus. "Oh?"

The boy's freckles were darkening against the white skin at the bridge of his nose and beads of sweat began to pop out along his hairline. His eyes narrowed. "It might be the one that Mister Cox used to have," he said. "The automotive classes worked on it? But Mister Cox says that truck died on him. He drove it after it got fixed at school but he says it died on him and then it got stolen." He looked at Peg and added, uneasily, "Mrs. Albright, Mister Albright's got a red truck, too, hasn't he? and he's pretty mad at Mister Bach? I guess you know."

Peg stared at him.

"Well, him and Mister Bach got into it? About Mister Albright using the school computers?"

Peg stood and looked at the kid but he had nothing more to say. He pulled away from her and headed back toward the waiting room. Peg followed him down the hall, wondering what Jerome had to do with Dobie's computers.

Kent Cox glanced up with an absent smile as Gilly and Peg came in. Peg sat, eyeing Kent, miserably sifting through what Gilly had said, wondering whether Kent Cox knew anything about Jerome and some computers at Dobie High, whether the detectives would confide in her. Probably not. Jerome worked on the A/C at the school, she thought, miserably, and shoved the thought away. Gilly was just a kid. Full of crazy kid talk.

Then, as she sat there, slightly sick to her stomach, Gilly's description of the guy who slugged Peter sank in and she looked around. What had the kid said? Hair "sort of like Mister Cox's"? Kent's hair was fading red, like salt and pepper. Sure wasn't dark. And Kent was Kent. Pathetic, over there, overweight, humped down into a chair too small for him. Always did look so sort of vulnerable and lonely, but who would date a man who smelled of dog? Another dog lover, maybe.

He must have ridden his bicycle over to the hospital. He'd come in with that silly bright blue helmet under his arm and took forever to put it down under his chair. Thinking of Kent slugging anybody was about as goofy as Lila Mae Bernathy's punching out somebody. Twittery little Lila Mae, over there. Peg had had her for Domestic Science, in her freshman year. Used to knock off grade points for the toilet tissue thing. Lila Mae had this theory that there had to be only one right way to put toilet tissue on a roller. Peg kept getting it wrong. You were supposed to have the paper sheet hanging out in front. All toilet tissue was to be installed with the loose side out, toward the hand, always and forever.

She had a strident voice, for such a little person. The noise level was going up but you could hear Lila Mae: "No excuse for a married man to be looking at that pornography," she was saying. "Especially in a high school. No excuse for it." She glanced up at Peg, looked away, and fell silent.

Old bat. Some people stayed pretty much the same through the years, Peg thought. Kent's first wife been a shrill little character, too. Delia. What a piece of work. Walked out on Kent right before Christmas, that year.

Lila Mae had Dobie's principal backed into a corner. Old C. J. Charles J. Markum. C.J. looked like he wanted out of there and away from Lila Mae in the worst way. Standing around with that sick smile. How they hanging, C.J.? I guess you had to show up, Peg thought, but who's gonna buy that sad look on your puss? Buckets of sweat between you and Pete. Like the thing with the beard. Peg had to smile, remembering Peter and the beard thing. Pete, telling her, "C.J. says I have to shave it off, 'or else'." "And?" "I told him to go ahead and 'or else' me," Peter said. So Peter kept the beard and went around wearing a big, day-glow, orange tin button: "Chuck you, Farley!" for years and years. Wore that button everywhere but to class and to Sunday School.

That beard got to be a regular gray and brown bush. Peter kept it right into December and powdered it to play Father Christmas in the children's show at the Pasadena Little Theater.

Come to think of it, that's when Kent Cox grew his beard, too, Peg realized. Kent always did follow Pete. Even had to grow a beard because Pete did. Peg shook her head.

"Penny for your thoughts," Kent asked. "You've got the wickedest grin."

"Ah, I'm just reminiscing," Peg said. "Remembering Peter and the time C.J. wanted him to shave off his beard. And then you grew one, too."

Kent tipped his head toward the principal, in a corner of the room. "Drove old C.J. nuts," he said, out of the side of his mouth.

"Oh, yeah," Peg said.

"God, this is awful," Kent said. "You think Hetty's going to be okay?" He wiped at brow and chin. "Mercy. Mercy."

Mercy. He made Peg smile. "You're the only straight guy I know who says that, like that," she told him. "I don't know. She's sure gonna need us."

Kent blinked, his hand over his mouth, his face going shiny beneath a rising blush. "I know."

"Yeah," Peg said. "Mercy." She turned closer and put her head down on his shoulder, briefly, and sat back with her eyes closed. How many years have you been in love with Hetty, she thought. Forever. Even before Delia left you and Pete and Hetty took you in. Poor baby. Standing around in the wings, with that hound dog look, all these years.

Later, when she was driving Hetty back to the house, Peg remembered how pink Kent got. "Kent Cox still blushes like a girl," she said. "Poor guy. Living up over that theater, all these years. Bicycling around all by his lonesome. Talking to that darned cow of a dog."

"Milo is a male," Hetty said.

"Looks like a big black cow, to me. Anyway. Poor Kent. Men never know what to do with themselves in a hospital, do they?" Peg went on. She reached over and gave Hetty's arm a gentle

The Field

squeeze. "We all love him, you know. Everybody. Everybody loves him."

Hetty nodded. She knew.

*

The next morning, Sunday, Hetty made herself sit down and go through some of the mail that had accumulated on the table in the front hall. Somebody, probably one of the Gofors, had been bringing in the mail and the paper. The Gofors had a key. So many people had keys to the house that Peter used to say there was no point in locking the door but it was a great convenience, having people have keys.

Hetty started her morning tea brewing and went into the study to get the checkbook in its cubbyhole in Peter's desk. She had to make herself realize that she would have to begin to pay attention to things like the mail and the bills. As that sank in, she found herself looking around at Pete's study through a blur of tears. All the polished surfaces were covered with a film of dust. Dust motes danced in a slant of light across the desk. Peter's desk. It used to be Peter's daddy's big roll topped desk, with the Norman Rockwell print of the child getting a vaccination in a silver frame. She could think what they'd done with that print. It didn't matter. She wiped at her eyes with the heels of her hands, wondering why the desk drawers were standing open. Peter kept everything in such good order. George Gordon never could understand Peter's passion for orderliness. He had a way of imitating Peter's voice: "A place for everything and everything in its place."

Everything was all out of place.

Oh, Peter will hate this, Hetty thought. Somebody's been rifling through his desk.

10

The next day, Peg had a fit when Hetty told her about the rifling of Peter's desk. She stood there looking at it, saying, "Did you call the police?"

"Of course."

"Well, that's it. You're not coming back to this house. You're not staying in this house another minute. You're moving in with me, changing all the locks and buying a pit bull," she said, yanking at her hair.

"Oh, Peg." What Hetty wanted, more than anything, was to get going to the hospital.

They barely made it in time for her first visit inside the unit.

The detectives arrived at the hospital a little before noon. Lieutenants Stephens and Gray led Hetty and Peg down the hall to a room with paint cans stacked along one wall and a long handled roller propped in one corner. Gray pulled a drop cloth off of a couch. As soon as Hetty sat and Peg plunked down next to her Lieut. Gray leaned toward them, his brow furrowed and his eyes intent. "Do you have any idea what someone might have been looking for?"

Hetty shook her head.

"I understand a number of people have keys to the house," he said. Hetty nodded again. Then he asked, very gently, if Hetty could give him a list of the people with access to the house and Peg couldn't contain herself.

"Oh, lots of luck. Be easier to try to figure out who doesn't have a key to Pete and Hetty's," she said.

"A few friends," Hetty murmured.

"And half a dozen neighbors," Peg said. "And former neighbors."

The Field

Lieut. Gray said, "The people who have had keys aren't necessarily people you have to assume are guilty of...of anything, Mrs. Bach. I don't mean to indicate that. I know how difficult this is." His voice dropped.

Hetty cleared her throat. "The Gofors see to Shadow, any time we take a trip or whatever." She looked at her hands, wishing all this talk could be over with, but the detective wasn't finished.

"Does Mr. Cox have a key?" he asked.

"I suppose so. Kent stayed with us, for a time."

Lieut. Gray consulted his notes. "Does Mr. Schmulbeck take care of your cat, from time to time?" His voice and a slight smile made the question unobtrusive.

Peg laughed. "Not likely," she said. "Johnny hates cats. He'll go out of his way to—"

"Oh, Peg," Hetty said. "Be careful with the truth. That's simply not so."

"It is too," Peg said. "Johnny's allergic. That whole family is. To everything. Johnny's wife can hardly leave the house. She's one of those. Hallie gets as far as the front door she breaks out with tremors and trembles unless Johnny or somebody begs and cajoles and about half carries her." She snorted. "If Johnny or Emily didn't go to the grocery, Hallie would just have to starve."

Hetty frowned at her.

"Well, I'm sorry," Peg said, not sounding at all sorry. "What if Johnny didn't bring home any groceries? You ever think about that? Hallie'd have to snap out of it, wouldn't she? Now that Emily's going off to SweetSue maybe she'll have to pull herself up by her bootstraps and get a grip."

"Peg," Hetty said.

"Well," Peg said. "Won't she? And Johnny does, too, hate cats. He says they're like rodents with fuzzy tails."

The detective was looking away, his face deliberately blank.

Hetty sighed. "Johnny has a key," she said, carefully. "Because he's our friend. Like Peg, here. We tend to make allowances." She sat back and took a breath and went on, "I'll try to make a list. Lila Mae Abernathy has a key." She took another longer breath, remembering. "From that time when her upstairs neighbor flooded her condominium."

The two men glanced at each other and sat looking at Hetty, waiting.

"The Gofors have been bringing in the mail for me," she said. "Did I tell you that? I think I did."

The lieutenant made a note in his notebook.

"You've met David," Hetty said. "Could you possibly see him as any sort of threat?"

"And you've met Louise, David's wife," Peg said. "The one with diamonds in her ears, at ten o'clock in the morning?"

"Peg," Hetty said. "The Gofors have been very helpful," she went on, enunciating precisely. "Dave or Louise or young Donald might not have been too careful about locking up after themselves. Some child might have gotten in and been, you know, looking for something in that desk. They might have wanted a pair of scissors or the paste, or whatever. It might not have anything to do with...with what's happened."

Peg got up and walked around the room. "She can't think straight," she said to the detectives. She came back to put her arms around Hetty. "Nobody expects you to think straight."

"So, the Gofor family, across the street, has a key," Lieut. Stephens said, clearing his throat. He stood and went over and looked down at the paint cans stacked along the wall. "And a number of your other friends."

"Kent Cox lived with Peter and Hetty for a while, after his wife Delia left him, and he was all destitute and depressed," Peg said. "Over one Christmas time and up until summer. When was that?"

Hetty shrugged.

"Anyway," Peg said. "Kent's probably still got his key. And there's that big kid with the noisy motorcycle that I wouldn't let anywhere near my house on a bet. Do you suppose he's got a key?"

She was being flippant but both the detectives looked intently alert. "Mister Van Huys?" When Lieut. Gray touched her hand, Hetty realized they were all waiting for her to say something. "No," she said. "Not Clifford. I don't suppose Clifford has a key. Unless...." She smiled faintly. "That might be moot. I don't doubt but what Clifford Van Huys could get into our house, if he wanted to."

"And that goes for his whole gang," Peg said.

The Field

The detectives glanced at each other.

"Any house," Peg said. She flipped her hair back. "Any time."

Hetty sat up. Something prickled at the back of her mind but she couldn't quite define it. "You don't suspect Clifford? Because it's my impression that he is very grateful to my husband. Peter helped Clifford before and after school, early and late. If you could see that young man when he was with Peter, well, I don't know how to make you understand how he—he truly wouldn't let anyone hurt Peter."

The detective repeated her last words with a quiet intensity that Hetty found unnerving. "Wouldn't let anyone hurt Peter?" He seemed to put a different slant on what she'd said.

She was suddenly weary. "Look. I'm sorry. Haven't we had enough surmising?" She stood up. "Aren't you tired of the scent of paint in here? These paint fumes might be bad for the baby, Peg." She took a tentative step toward the door. "Are we finished?"

Lieut. Gray stood up. "Of course."

Hetty shook her head. "I'm...I'm sorry I can't seem to be more helpful."

"Perfectly understandable," the detective said. "Well, somewhere down the line, we'll talk about this some more when it's a bit easier."

It won't be easier, Hetty thought. But then she remembered something. "Peter told me that a youngster cried in his classroom, the last day of school. He came in late for supper and he wasn't very hungry."

She looked away, trying to remember. "Everybody leans on Peter." She frowned with the effort of explaining. "He's just so good. His father was like that, too." It made her have to stop talking and wipe her eyes and nose. "It's a family trait. I'm sorry I'm so weepy."

"I know this has to be hard, ma'am. But you never know what might give us some kind of a handle on this thing," the detective said.

Hetty said, "Peter doesn't like to talk about some of these things. He's...Peter is a big respecter of kid-teacher confidentiality. Kids come to him with all kinds of things. He's had to break it to parents that they were going to become grandparents. He's had to help girls break up those clubs where they have to shoplift to get in. He took it upon himself to tell someone working at Dobie to look for another job when he discovered he'd been looking at pornography on the school computers. Peter is just so good. Everything, everyone is so important to him." She couldn't go on.

"Yes." The detective smiled. The smile didn't reach his eyes and it didn't last long.

"The student who cried might have been some teenager in terrible trouble," Hetty said. "High school is an awful time for so many youngsters."

"Yes." The man sighed.

"I don't even know if it was a girl or a boy."

The detective looked as exhausted as Hetty felt. He got up and walked along with her down the hall. "You may know more than you think you do."

"I'll try," Hetty said. Her voice quavered and she brought it back under control. "I will."

They were almost back at the waiting room when Peg asked, "Have you gotten anywhere with the license plate on that truck?"

"We're on that," Lieut. Stephens said.

Hetty said, "I've never paid any attention to people's automobiles or trucks. Once when my friends had a surprise party they had the guests drive all over the subdivision to hide their cars and then they all laughed thinking about how out of it I am. They could have parked right out in front of the house and I'd never notice. I just never have paid attention to...to such things."

It was time for Hetty to be let into the unit for one of her ten minute visits.

As soon as Hetty'd left them, Peg turned to the detectives and said, "I can't believe you haven't gotten somewhere with that truck license."

"Well, the last time I tried to talk about that with Mrs. Bach she got so upset we dropped it. There was a red pickup Mazda truck registered to Mister Cox; plate number seven, eight, one, MEO. But Mister Cox no longer has it."

"Good grief," Peg sputtered. "There's a dead end. I thought it was a Ford."

"The Mazdas and the Fords were identical, that year," the detective said. "Made the same, everything the same. Same truck. Different name."

"Oh," Peg said. "So the guy who slugged Peter might have been driving a Mazda? Or he might have been driving that Ford truck that Dave gave Kent Cox so his high school automotive classes could play with it?"

"Entirely possible. But it seems to have disappeared. Mister Cox says it was stolen. He thinks some kids took it joy-riding and it died on them. It was of so little value he never bothered to report it. He tells us it was taken from the school lot but he'd decided it wasn't worth getting some youngster in trouble over."

Peg looked around. "So that's why you're curious about Kent?" Lieut. Gray's eyebrows lifted.

"Well. I mean. Kent Cox. Gee. If you can't do better than that." He looked more askance.

"If you knew Kent," Peg said. "Casper Milquetoast. Besides, didn't he say that he was up at Lake Livingston over the holiday?"

"That's what he says," Lieut. Gray said, carefully. He glanced at his colleague before he turned back to ask Peg, "All by himself. At the lake. All weekend."

"Well, he does that kind of thing," Peg said. "Kent's a tree hugger. The Gofors have this cabin up in Hawg Heaven they let him use. It's got a little mobile home on one end of a lot up in the woods near the lake. He takes that big black lab of his up there and they romp around looking at alligator's eyes on the surface of the lake or sit around watching squirrels. Sometimes Kent looks a little squirrelly, with that timid smile and the big front teeth over that under bite of his, but he's got to be harmless enough. If that's where he said he was, that's where he was."

She rubbed her back. "It would kill Hetty to think of Kent's being under suspicion. He isn't, actually, is he?"

When the detectives didn't say anything she went on, "Just because of the truck?"

Neither of them seemed to want to answer. After a couple of minutes Lieut. Stephens said, "We ought to be getting back downtown."

They wouldn't say any more. Peg was kind of glad to see them leave. She watched them trudge down the hall thinking, come on, guys, take it easy on poor old Kent, of all people. He's got problems enough.

Peg got Jerome to change the locks and put chains on the inside of Hetty's front and back doors but Peg still wanted her to come and live with her.

*

On Monday night, Hetty insisted on driving herself home. Peg followed and went straight to the kitchen to open a can of soup, saying, "You have to eat."

Shadow was furious at being neglected. He wouldn't come near either of them. He walked around stiff-legged with his ears flattened and his eyes narrowed, sounding off.

Peg said she couldn't blame him. She heated up chicken noodle soup in the microwave and moved about Hetty's house, putting out fresh food and water for Shadow, watering her scheffelera and ivies that were beginning to droop.

"If you'd just come home with me," Peg said. "New locks or not, I don't want to leave you here. Besides, my mom won't pick on me as much if you're there."

Hetty said she needed her own bed.

After Peg left, Hetty tried to eat some of the soup. It tasted like salty tears.

She gave it up and went into the living room. There was a magazine with a big eye on the cover on one of the end tables. It reminded her of the tattered magazines at the hospital. It made her sigh to think of all those outdated magazines in all those waiting rooms all over that hospital; all those wretched turquoise rooms, full of people leafing through magazines, all day and all night. Women, mostly. Women in waiting, sick with worry.

All that had been going on all while she had been so unaware; so happily concerned with the busy-ness of living, for so long.

Nobody actually reads hospital magazines, she thought. What they are looking at goes to some level inside and rides around for a while and gets kicked back out.

A magazine could get to looking peculiar. Especially the advertisements. Cars. Furniture. Perfume. Most of it just...trash. Nothing. Nothing of any genuine worth, nothing that could do anything, mean anything, truly help anyone. Very very little of the things in

The Field

those ads would ever have anything to do with anybody like her or her Peter, who never did care what he wore, who would go off in loafers and no socks, half the time, if she didn't catch him.

Hetty, crying, found herself gazing at a photograph of a sofa floating above cumulus clouds, a part of her thinking, numbly, yes, yes, that's a good place for a red leather sofa, right up there in the blue, blue sky. She came across a dark page with a shiny stroke of red across it and sat and looked at it for several seconds before it came to her that what she was gazing at was an enlargement of a mouth. A tube of lipstick drawing a shiny mouth. To sell a tube of red grease. Of course. Ah, but what might the mouth be trying to say?

Eyes. The next page had eyes, with long, black, curved eyelashes mirrored in their depths.

Grotesque.

Maybe the greasy mouth was talking about eyes. She could hear Peter. "That youngster has her dad's eyes. I've got to get him to see what he's doing to her." When had he said that? When he was telling her where he'd be, that last thing, on Memorial Day? Why hadn't she paid attention? She got up, tossed the magazine in the trash and went upstairs.

She was in the shower when she remembered. It had been that day. While he was getting dressed. Peter was talking to her, standing with his knees apart, using his knees to hold his pants up so he could tuck in his shirt, when he glanced in the mirror and said something about meeting someone because he had to help him get straightened out about something.

After he'd gotten zipped up, he buckled his belt and leaned closer to the glass and started saying something about this student, who'd cried, who'd come to see him after school and had cried in his classroom and...and the kid had been all upset about something having to do with her dad.

Hetty's eyes hurt. Her throat hurt. Everything hurt.

She toweled off, got into bed and stretched out.

Shadow bounded to her chest, forgiving her.

"It's all right to be mad," Hetty told him. "I wish I could get mad. It might help."

She watched a frieze of moonlit leaf-patterns move across the ceiling until the first false dawn glazed the windows.

*

The next day, a Tuesday, Peter was much worse. He looked even more gaunt, the skin tight against his jaw and neck. The translucent tubes snaked out from under the sheets. The screen up behind the head of the bed kept its bright pulsing line. Hetty touched his peeling lower lip with a glycerin swab, praying that somewhere, somewhere within himself he could know that she was with him.

He was letting go. The psyche or the soul or whatever...his mind? His wonderful mind was leaving. Letting go. Pete used to make a joke, he'd tease, sometimes, when she got exasperated with him for being so absent-minded. She'd scold him and he'd say, "Don't hold back." And if she got fierce, he'd cock an eyebrow and ask: "But how do you really feel about that?" and, sometimes, with a little rap at her brow, "So, how does the cauliflower feel about that?" meaning her brain, what he liked to refer to as the cauliflower in the skull.

He was so hurt. What was in there now was so...so hurt. Bruised. That couldn't be all there was to him, though. It couldn't be. Because it was...leaving. Her Pete, who nuzzled her, who slid his long arms around her and gathered her to him every night, every night, who would hold her where she belonged, in the hollow of his shoulder, her Pete, that she leaned down across the back of the recliner to hold was going away.

One of the nurses came over to stand beside her and touch her on the shoulder when her time was up. When Hetty looked up at her the woman eyes were so sadly sympathetic that Hetty's heart constricted and started to pound hurtfully. She got up and walked stiffly out of the unit and went back into the waiting room with her throat aching.

She tried to push the misery of being so scared away but it moved coldly, sickeningly all through her because she knew.

She knew.

She was sitting very upright on the sofa, trying not to cry in front of all the people in the waiting room when the Indian doctor came out and stood looking at her.

He led her back to his office and leaned against a wall, his shoulders rounded and his dark eyes half closed. "It's over," he said. "We've lost him." He crouched down in front of Hetty and squinted at her until she put her hands out for him to take. "We've lost him. I am so very sorry, Mrs. Bach."

After a couple of seconds he let go of her hands and stood in front of her, lifting his arms and letting them drop, his hands slapping his thighs in helpless frustration. "Ah, you've just got to hate this," he said. "You see this, you keep seeing this and you've got to hate it. This waste. You want someone to help you to understand it, to figure it out." He slapped the sides of his legs and sighed in bitter exhaustion. "But you can't, you know. You simply cannot."

"Maybe I have to," Hetty said, her throat so clogged with tears that the doctor couldn't possibly understand her.

It didn't matter if he understood. She wasn't talking to him.

11

The Funeral

The funeral was on a Friday. June Seventh. Two o'clock in the afternoon. The hottest part of a long hot day.

Peg wasn't drunk but she certainly wasn't sober. She stumbled, sun-blinded and slightly off balance from the heat of the parking lot, as she and Hetty and George Gordon entered the dim, cool, gardenia scented foyer of the funeral chapel at Forest Park East.

George Gordon pressed Hetty's arm tightly to his side and gave Peg a minute to right herself. "Now, then," he said. "Now, then. Chin up." Then he almost lost his footing. He kicked the edge of a carpeted step and staggered for a couple of seconds.

"Watch it, guys," Peg muttered. "If I land on my back we're gonna need a crane and derrick and a two strand pulley to get me right side up and I don't think they could get through that parking lot."

Peg had fortified herself with what was left of the big fat bottle of Scotch Jerome had stashed in the back of the pantry. She had drunk Scotch in the middle of the day exactly once before in her entire life; when she had come home from trying to teach Sunday School to a high school class at the Unitarian Church. Today, when she couldn't stop crying, even after she'd used up all the hot water in the shower, she had gotten out Jerome's Scotch.

It did seem to smooth things out, some.

Everybody in town is here, she thought, looking around the chapel, watching Kent Cox shoulder his way through the crowd to lead them to their chairs. Everybody and his cousin. I hope they have some way to broadcast the service to the overflow crowd baking out there in that melting parking lot.

I am not going to cry, she vowed.

A tall man with a square jaw was talking to Kent and David, at the front of the room. Peg didn't recognize him. "Is that your minister?" she asked Hetty. Hetty frowned, dazed. She turned to Peg and followed her eyes.

"Yes."

"Unitarian?"

"Yes."

"He looks like Sean Connery," Peg muttered.

"No," Hetty said.

"Doesn't that man with the profile look like Sean Connery?" Peg asked George Gordon.

George Gordon, still a bit teetery, let go of her arm and took a firmer grip with his other hand. "I beg your pardon?"

"The minister It's remarkable. Look."

George Gordon looked.

Peg mistook George Gordon's hard squeeze for assent. "Remarkable, don't you think?"

"No," George Gordon said.

"Oh," Peg said. "Well. Sit down then." Old fool, she thought. What does he know?

She was determined to not weep. I'm all cried out, she told herself. I'm all cried out, and Hetty's got to get through this and I'm not even going to listen to whatever it is that Kent's got all written out, that he's going to hold in his shaking cold hands, up there. Kent is the least articulate of the whole bunch of us and it's not fair for him to have to do this, bet or no bet. He looks like he's going to fall to his knees and roll around sobbing any minute.

There was no coffin. Peter had been quite specific about that. There was an urn and Peter's portrait, on the easel, off to the right and slightly behind the podium. The portrait wasn't a very recent one. Peter hadn't had room in his life for a lot of sitting around and posing for the portrait camera. "Vanity," he'd said. "Vanity, vanity, all is vanity," whenever Hetty had tried to browbeat him into having his picture taken.

Peg could hear Peter, hear his staccato chuckle and see his lopsided smile, as he said that.

The funeral director had to step forward and tap Kent on the arm and even then poor Kent couldn't seem to get himself together. He startled and blushed and hurried up to the podium and stood there, perspiration gleaming on his shiny brow. "Like most of you, I've known Peter Bach well and long," he said, pausing to shuffle through his notes. "Our Peter is one of God's chosen gentlemen, isn't he?" and for a long uneasy couple of minutes Peg thought he might be going to give up and sit down.

He groaned and peered out and around over his reading glasses, took them off, stuck them in his shirt pocket, looked down at his notes, crumpled them into a wad and let them drop. "Shoot. I've been trying to put this together but it's hopeless." He drew a long breath that broke in the middle.

Oh, come on, Kent, Peg thought. If you're going to do this, do it. Grow up. The longer he stood there, quaking, the more Kent looked like the fat freckled kid with the big teeth, forever panting along behind, telling the gang to wait up, trying to catch up and never quite making it. How could Delia walk out on such a puppy-person? Good thing he'd had Hetty and Peter to carry him through that.

Brought it on himself, though, in a way. Squirrelly Kent. In love with Hetty Bach and marrying a woman like Delia. Some substitute. Delia wasn't a bit like Hetty. Delia was dippy Delia, with the Betty Davis eyes, drifting around with a cigarette, burning little holes in all her drifty outfits, with all that unwashed red hair and that peachy British complexion that's got to be a mess of wrinkles by now if she's still smoking as much as she used to.

If only he'd stand up straight, Peg thought, and made an effort to sit taller.

"Shoot." Kent said, with a sad little moan. He mopped his brow and looked around. "Peter started teaching the year after I did." He paused, remembering. "That first day, Lila Mae Bernathy walked over to him and told him the same thing she told me on my first day: 'We have a rule here, Mister Bach. You don't smile until Christmas.'" He peered around myopically. "That's the way we saw it, right, Lila Mae?"

He paused and cleared his throat. "I don't think he ever did get the message on that." He shrugged. "If you're a smiler, you're a smiler, I guess. Pete's dad was like that, too. Peter's dad could sit in a room full of people and not say a word and after a while everybody in that room would be turning to him like to a... to the morning sun.

"My old man did the eulogy at Peter's folks' funeral and I have to say he did a much better job than I'm doing. That was in this chapel right here. Right after the worst Valentine's Day any of us ever saw. But I didn't mean to get into that." He looked around.

"Back then Hetty was kind of like a little sister to our boy." He looked at Hetty and tried to smile. "Turned out our Pete never did get serious about anybody else. Guess he was meant for Hetty all along." He swallowed. "Eternally."

His chin sank to his chest and he ruminated, for a couple of seconds and got out a handkerchief to wipe his eyes and nose. "When Peter and Hetty got married, the night before the wedding—well, it was more toward morning when we were all a little bit under the weather—Peter asked me, right out, 'Hey, man, are you in love with my lady?' and I said, 'Isn't everybody?' Because everybody was. Is. Aw, I'm rambling, here. Lost all track of myself. I was going to say something about how he's got to be the best teacher Dobie ever had or ever will have, and how many times old Pete walked off with the Golden Apple Favorite Teacher award and some of that. But I can't seem to bring myself, since those of us who never will get a crack at one of those might find that subject a little tiresome, and there was Pete, keeping those things in the garage with all the rest of his awards and plaques that he always referred to as his 'plagues' because sometimes they made him make some speeches."

Some of the faculty made chuckling noises, agreeing with him, and Kent looked up, encouraged. "And I was going to talk about how Peter Bach was the sweetest guy and the best friend, except for this one time I got the chicken pox and he had to take my place in the melodrama and he came over with some ice cream and sat around making me promise to do this eulogy which I figured would never happen because I figured Peter would have to outlive me, because anybody so many people need and love ought to live forever. But it turns out I don't especially want to talk about that either. Because I can't."

He drew a shaky breath and went on, his voice strained, "Just meant to say, we all loved the guy and he loved us back, and Hetty, well, Hetty, you're good folks, good, good people, the best I know of. And that's good because, well, our boy deserved every good thing, didn't he? And now maybe I better sit down if I'm gonna stand around sniveling. God's chosen gentleman, he was, our Pete, wasn't he?"

Kent left the podium with his mouth tight and his shoulders hunched.

The minister took over. He began by calmly agreeing with Kent's remark about Pete's being one of God's chosen gentlemen. "Know ye not that there is a prince and great man fallen this day in Israel?" he said and people started sobbing. Peg dug her fingernails into her arms and let herself look at Hetty's face and that did it. She started to cry. She'd been fighting this off too hard and there she was, suddenly sick with sorrow. She couldn't bear it, couldn't bear to see Hetty like this, in here, with all these crying people, in this gardenia scented crowded room. The words *fallen* and *this day* echoed and squeezed her heart all the way shut.

"A prince and a great man." Yes.

Peg looked over at Hetty and tried to stop crying. Hetty looked...killed.

The minister closed the Bible and stepped down.

Kent got up again, then, and said, "There's some maps that show the way to Het's house, if anybody here needs a map. Dave Gofor and his good wife, Louise, have some maps for you, or you can follow the caravan."

As people began to get to their feet, Peg, waiting for George Gordon to pull himself together and tuck his handkerchief in his pocket, tried to get herself under control by scanning the room. Johnny Schmulbeck looked over at her, his face shining with tears, and turned back to gather Hallie in and cup her head to his chest. They stood, swaying, backlit by the sun's rays slanting through the burgundy and gold of a stained glass window.

Then Johnny turned to lean toward a big youngster Peg didn't recognize, a dark youngster in what looked like the expensively casual draping of an Armani suit. Johnny was turned away from her so Peg couldn't see the expression on his face but the young man's face looked so chillingly blank that she couldn't look away.

Why, that boy is furious, she thought. He's livid. And Johnny is confronting him, standing there with both his fists clenched.

David Gofor moved in the way, then, shepherding his chubby daughter, Doris, and saying something to young Donald, moving along with the Gilbreath youngster and another boy whose braces glinted in the late afternoon sunlight.

Peg let herself be led through the crowd by George, with Hetty behind her. Mourners milled around the paved and sheltered area adjacent to the blacktopped parking lot outside the chapel, some of them on their way to their cars and some, sweating in dark clothes in the June heat, edging up to murmur farewell condolences.

Peg and Hetty had to wait, in the motionless, hot, bright air, for what felt like hours, as George Gordon went bumbling in circles looking for the car. The milling crowd receded into a kind of distant silence as Peg gazed around. Some of the youngsters in the crowd had the mottled, bright-eyed look of an impending outburst but their voices stayed hushed.

How they loved him, Peg thought, even the kids. Especially the kids. Tears pricked at her eyes.

She was fighting for control again, seeing through a blur, as Johnny and Hallie and Emily walked to the exit end of the lot. And there was the big kid in the Armani suit, pacing quickly, gracefully, weaving in and out of the crowd, to get to them. The kid moved like a dancer, Peg thought. Like a Spanish dancer, with the crowd parting to make way. He came up to Johnny and Hallie, stopped and stood squarely in front of them. Johnny's timid little wife cowered inside his protectively encircling arm.

Peg knew she was staring but she couldn't look away.

The big kid bowed and offered Emily his arm.

Emily took it.

Emily turned away from her mother and dad and tucked her hand into the crook of that huge kid's left arm.

Peg couldn't believe it.

Then things got even more unbelievable. That kid led Emily over to a huge, shiny, black, Harley Davidson motorcycle. And Emily climbed aboard the thing.

That whole demented episode, the way Johnny and Hallie

looked, helplessly, hopelessly standing there, the way the kid looked, big and, God, imposing, but bad, with those black sunglasses, that whole thing was such a shock that it lifted Peg, momentarily, out of her misery.

It was just so amazing.

Johnny's overly protected cherished darling, Emily, in her lace and ribbons, taking off, like that, on a crazy motorcycle, in front of God and everybody.

Weird, the things that stick in a person's head. The last thing Peg would remember about that wretched Friday, June Seventh, the day of Peter Bach's funeral service in that chapel with that huge suffering crowd, was the noisy rumble of a motorcycle going down the feeder road and turning onto the Gulf freeway—vroom vroom—-barreling up the pike toward Galveston.

Good God, Peg thought. We're going to have to shoot Johnny to put him out of his misery and lock Hallie away in one of those homes for the perpetually bewildered. They'll never make it through this.

12

George Gordon drove slowly. The fields alongside the freeway shimmered in waves of heat.

Hetty's house filled almost at once and a good many mourners stayed for hours. Kent Cox apologed for not doing the eulogy very well. He had too much to drink and kept apologizing right up until he went wobbling out to his car. Then there was a flurry of voices outside, with various people deciding who should drive Kent home and the arranging of cars and so forth. Groups of people stood around deciding these things in the driveway while Hetty stood in the doorway of her house, in the slanting red and gold rays of the setting sun, watching, watching, through a kind of fog.

As the crowd thinned, she watched Peg go around turning on lamps, the two lamps on the wall next to the fireplace, the standing lamp behind Peter's recliner and Hetty's reading lamp with its pale parchment shade. The downstairs took on its familiar peachy evening glow. Peg neglected to close the blinds and the windows became discordantly dark but Hetty told herself the black of the windows didn't matter. She'd close the blinds herself in a moment.

Or not. Possibly not.

She sat in an unfocused haze, nodding as Peg turned on her lamps and, later, hearing people murmur as they left, by twos and threes. Then she watched Louise and Lila Mae and George Gordon gather up dips and platters of sliced meat going iridescent on limp lettuce leaves. They wouldn't let her help.

The room smelled faintly of food and wine and cigarettes. David and Louise always made it a point to step out on the veranda to light up but the living room smelled faintly of smoke just the same. It didn't seem a particularly bad odor. It was just there. Like Lila

Mae's Chanel Number Five and George Gordon's minty cologne. Definitely there.

Like Lila Mae's chirping and Louise Gofor's incessant voice. When Hetty got up and went into the kitchen, she sat down in her rocker and rocked a bit, half aware of Louise's voice in the kitchen in a kind of undercurrent, point, counterpoint, to Lila Mae, in the dining room. "It's been ever so long since we've all been together," Louise was saying. "The boys see each other all the time but what is it with us, that we're so busy? We need to try to get together more often, don't you think? I mean, you never know. Life is so uncertain. And...and short." She looked up and noticed that Peg was gazing at her and her voice trailed off.

Lila Mae came into the kitchen and said, "Oh, there you are, dear," to Hetty. "I rather imagine Hetty's had quite enough of all of us for a spell," she announced, her mouth in the tight little smile that she had, now, since the stroke. "I'll be running along, dear," she said to Hetty. "I hope you're able to rest, this night."

She glanced at Louise. "It was a lovely service. Even the youngsters were moved. The Gilbreath boy and young Chaney and your Donald, Louise. Good to see these young men paying their respects. Even Van Huys boy came. I think these things have an effect."

Peg looked up. "An effect?"

Lila Mae looked flustered.

"Do you know the Van Huys boy?" Peg asked.

Lila Mae nodded. "Clifford Van Huys. The one with the motorcycle. He's still a student. He's not in my classes but I know of him, yes." She emphasized the "of" and peered at Hetty, confidingly. "He's been very kind to a friend of mine who's been very ill. Scarcely a scholar, but there's a lot of potential there. Just not what you'd call much motivated. The father's very well-to-do. He's in one of those pyramid scheme businesses, up in Michigan, I'm told. Amway, or one of those. An entrepreneur. But nobody wants to know what goes on in that house that boy's left alone in. And he tools around on that Harley. Most of the boys give him a wide berth but some of the girls...well." She shrugged and rolled her eyes. "You'd be surprised at how many young ladies find a motorcycle exciting."

Peg had come close and overheard that. "That so?" she asked.

Lila Mae looked annoyed. "I just said it was so, didn't I?"

"Oops," Peg said, and ducked away.

Hetty walked Lila Mae to the door and, as she stepped outside, Lilia Mae tapped her on the arm and leaned close, to say, softly, "Why is that husband of Peggy's sitting out in your driveway, do you know? I hope his air conditioning is functioning. He hasn't been bothering you, has he? I understand those detectives are investigating him."

Hetty stepped outside and peered at the driveway. Jerome was slouched at the wheel of his pickup, one hand holding a cigarette hanging out of the window. Had he been out here all during the wake? He looked disconsolate. "He must be wanting to talk with Peg," she said

She walked across the lawn and lifted a hand in greeting. "Jerome, you must come in."

"Aw, that's okay," he said. "I'm in my work clothes. Just thought I'd see if Peggy was here. Sorry I didn't get to the service. I meant to, but I got a call. Every A/C in town is going full tilt already. Hope yours is okay." His voice changed. "Are you going to be all right? Anything you need, or anything? The locks working?"

"I'm all right. You needn't worry about your work clothes," Hetty said. "Do come in."

"Naw," he said. "That's okay."

Lila Mae was still on the front walk, listening, her head to one side. "Now don't you be worrying about that rascal," she said. "And don't you let people keep you up all this night. My, that Louise likes to talk, doesn't she? Hetty, you might want to be careful about letting people have keys to the house, now that you're alone. I've learned about that." She studied Hetty's face and her own face pulled down in sympathy. "Oh, dear. You ought to be in bed. Good night, dear."

When Hetty came back into the kitchen she beckoned to Peg. "Jerome's out on the drive. In this heat. Tell him to come in, if you like."

Peg went to the window over the sink and looked out and smiled. "Let him roast."

Hetty heard Peg but Louise couldn't hear anyone. Louise had so much to say she sometimes talked on an indrawn breath. "And

Johnny Schmulbeck has been going around insisting that tattooed biker has been stalking his darling Emily, though you know Johnny. Any male who so much as looks in her direction would have to be stalking his precious child, wouldn't he? Keeping her cooped up like that, why, it ought to be illegal. It's unnatural, to say the least."

Peg leaned against the sink. "Well, think about it," she said, genially. "A tattooed biker? Got to be Johnny's worst nightmare." She kept looking out the window over the sink, smiling to herself, as Louise went on, "Those detectives have been talking to every single body at Dobie High. They act like Kent Cox might be some kind of felon and they're looking into everything there is to know about Johnny Schmulbeck, is that insane?"

Peg wended her clumsy way past Louise for a stack of plates on the sideboard. "Johnny and Hallie are having a rough time."

Louise said, "Johnny and Hallie are always having a rough time. Hallie's a piece of work. She chose that place way out there in the boonies and now he can't get her out of the house. She won't even learn how to drive. Look at Hetty, she's had to learn how to shift and everything else, with that old Chevy." She turned to look at Hetty and her voice dropped a notch. "Different strokes, though, right? John Glenn's wife was this terribly shy little person when those astronauts lived over there in El Lago and now she's gotten completely over it."

"Might help if Johnny were an astronaut," Peg said, her eyes round. "Or a senator."

"Oh, you're so smart," Louise said. "But I mean it. Hallie's been coming apart for years and now Johnny is, too. Johnny's coming apart. He just *sits*."

Peg gazed out the window. "Jerome is leaving," she said, dreamily. "Isn't that a shame?" No one was listening to her.

"Well, I haven't been out to the Schmulbeck's in years," Louise went on, "but David drove over to Hitchcock last month to take pictures of that volunteer fire department for the paper and he invited himself over to Johnny's house and made the mistake of trying to talk that man into letting that bashful little Emily come back with him to go see a movie or something with Donald and the Chaney boy and Johnny got just awful." She stopped for a breath and shook her head. "Here, let me take those," she said to Peg, edging her away from the sink.

"Dave said it was awful. He ran into a brick wall. Johnny got terribly upset and soon as he left the room Hallie went on and on about how Johnny is simply grieving himself to death at the thought of Emily's going off to college. The very idea that she might go off to San Marcos or Nacogdoches or Austin is just sending him right over the edge."

She raised her voice above the clatter of silver in the sink. "David said Johnny just sits," she said.

"We all do too much of that," Peg said. She was wiping off the stove with her back to Louise.

"No, what I mean is, he just sits," Louise said, emphatically. She sat down in a chair and slumped, vacant-eyed, demonstrating. "He sits and stares at the TV with the sound off. All the time. We've all tried to help those two."

Peg turned around and faced Louise.

"Well, we have," Louise said. "Haven't we? All of us."

"So?" Peg murmured.

"Well, that poor child is her daddy's whole life. She's bound to be neurotic, cooped up with those two. I think she's already anorexic or asthmatic or something."

Peg had her hand on her hip. "Hell of a combination," she said. "No eating and no breathing."

"Well, you know what I mean," Louise said. "You'd think she might be planning to be going off to jail or a concentration camp or something instead of just to college." Louise was opening drawers. "Are there any more dry towels?"

Peg looked around. "We're about through, I think." She put a plate in the dishwasher and straightened up, drying her hands on her apron. "Maybe Johnny's remembering how sweet Sweetsue was when he was in San Marcos. Everybody knows it's a party school. They have T-shirts in the gift shop saying, 'Best seven years I ever had.'"

Louise sniffed. "Some of us got through in four years. Anyway, Emily has to get out into the world as soon as possible." She tucked her hair back and turned to Hetty. "You're going to have to be very careful until those nice detectives figure out what's happening around here, dear. I'm so glad you had the locks changed."

When Peg went back into the living room, Louise came closer to Hetty to add, under her breath, "That husband of Peg's may be no bargain but he is a fixer, isn't he? Did Jerome change your locks? Our air conditioner quit and Jerome came over on the holiday, Memorial Day in the afternoon, to fix it, just that quick. He might be a nice person if he weren't such a big old flirt. He is handsome, though, isn't he? With that go-to-hell grin and those eyes!"

She batted her lashes and licked her upper lip.

Someone turned on the television. The ten o'clock news came on before Peg left. Louise walked across the street soon after that, the last guest to leave.

George Gordon had dozed off on the sofa. Hetty dropped a quilt over him, turned off the TV and went upstairs to her bed.

*

The next day, George Gordon went home and got some clothes and moved in on Hetty, saying, "Now hasn't it always been the dream of our hearts to care for each other?" and "I can stay as long as you need me, angel. Now that it's just us, I guess I won't feel bad about using that guest room."

But four days later, on Tuesday morning, Hetty woke up to find him rummaging in the pantry, querulously complaining that he couldn't figure out where she kept the coffee. When she said there wasn't any he went trundling out to his car. An hour later he called to say that the grass needed cutting at his house. About four in the afternoon he called to say he'd decided to take a nap. "You'll be all right, Angel, won't you? Right as rain?"

"Fine as silk," Hetty said, completing the litany, but she was out of coffee and cat food and milk. She got dressed and got into the Ford and turned the key. The key clicked a hopeless small click. Peter had said something about the alternator in the Ford.

Okay, I can do this, she told herself. Clara's a much better car anyway.

She'd thought that Clara might take some getting used to but she was okay. She just felt like...Clara. Comfortable and safe.

Peter had loved working on Clara. What a lot of doing it had taken to convert her to a stick shift. He'd been so triumphant at succeeding. "Got rid of her three on a tree, honey," he'd called out. And Kent with him, caroling, "Four on the floor! Way to go!" A

The Field

good Saturday, that was, with Peter's hand over hers on this stick, his warm voice telling her, "You know you can do it. Think of an H, up to the left, down to the middle bar of the H..." with Kent chortling in the back seat, "Kinda like Zen. Chevrolet Zen."

A lifetime ago.

Kroger's still had some green plastic pots and baskets of stemmy plants on tables just inside the door. They looked so tired and sad that Hetty started to put them in her basket to resuscitate but the tight, buttony, little buds they were shedding made her throat ache.

A woman jerking a basket free from the chain of baskets said, to a small balding man beside her, "Don't forget the black olives." The man turned to the woman with his face creased in a patient smile and said to Hetty, "I never forget the olives." He gave the woman a brief husbandly hug. The pair looked so contented, so sure of themselves and each other that Hetty walked past them quickly, the lump in her throat getting bigger.

A man and woman at the meat counter were having a friendly argument about steaks. "As long as you're barbecuing anyway," the woman said, "why not these?" "I'm not wasting mesquite on anything less than top sirloin," the man answered, and got a wifely pat on the cheek. "Whatever," the woman said. She smiled at Hetty and Hetty realized that the woman was someone she ought to know, from the Art League or Emerson or somewhere. "We've been in the Colorado house," the woman said, smiling absently. "So gorgeous out there in the mountains. How's that big handsome husband of yours? Happy school's out?"

"Fine," Hetty heard herself say. "Thank you." She swallowed and walked away fast.

She got as far as the parking lot and started to make herself turn around and go back into the store but then she decided she was darned if she wanted to stand around in Kroger's with her eyes and nose dripping. She got in Clara and drove home.

Peg or George Gordon could go get Shadow some cat food or there might be some tuna in the pantry.

When she got home George Gordon was waiting in the kitchen, with Peg, the two of them being so excruciatingly frostily polite to each other that it was obvious that they must have been bickering. They wanted to discuss the fact that Hetty shouldn't go on living by herself. "Plenty of room at my place," George Gordon said.

"Oh, fine," Peg said.

"My dear," George Gordon said.

Peg rolled her eyes. "We could help each other out," she told Hetty. "Couldn't we? This is a great time to sell a house. You could probably make a nice profit on this place, get out from under the payments, and we can share expenses. We might even decide to go into some kind of business together. Clean houses or open a day care center. Take care of little kids. Groom poodles, maybe? How hard could it be to learn how to groom poodles?"

Hetty didn't want to groom poodles. What she wanted was to be left alone, in her own house. She went to the refrigerator, pried loose some of the foil wrapped frozen dinners crammed in the freezer and suggested Peg and George Gordon might want to take them along home before they thawed.

As soon as she had her house back, she opened a can of salmon, dumped it into Shadow's dish and went upstairs to bed.

*

All through June, the house was alternately empty and crowded. Hetty discovered that she was most often most lonely when there were too many people around.

The last week of June, Peg said Jerome told the boys he was going to take flying lessons. "Says he's going to be a crop duster pilot. You believe that? And Kevin says Pamela puts chocolate chips and whipped cream on pancakes." Peg didn't see how Jerome could afford flying lessons when he kept getting behind in his child support, though Hetty didn't think crop dusting sounded any crazier than some of Peg's mad entrepreneurial schemes.

On the Fourth of July, Peg had Kevin and Paul get down their old bunk bed from the attic, which was a regular furnace, and help her set it up so they could share one bedroom. The boys helped her paint the other two bedrooms with some acrylic paint she had in the garage. The walls were varying shades but the rooms didn't look half bad, she said. "And the ad in the Southbelt Courier under 'rooms for rent' only cost eight dollars."

Hetty wasn't sure that painting walls was such a great idea at this stage of the game for Peg. Her feet were so swollen she couldn't wear anything but Jerome's old moccasin bedroom slippers. She kept shuffling into Hetty's kitchen in those fat furry slippers to sit rubbing her back against the slats of the chair, tweaking at her hair. She kept tugging at hanks of her hair, winnowing out strands to slide through her fingers. Sometimes she pulled some right out.

Kent Cox kept calling, wanting to know if Hetty needed anything. Johnny wanted to know if Hetty needed anything. David and Louise Gofor kept asking if Hetty needed anything. People from the Water Color Society and Art League and Women in the Visual and Literary Arts and Emerson Unitarian church kept calling and coming over, wanting to know if Hetty needed anything.

Missy Fredericks, who taught math at Dobie High, somebody Hetty had always thought of as pleasant enough, came over on a Saturday with three women in tow, to deliver another Stouffer's frozen lasagna. When Missy had trouble fitting the lasagna into the freezer she accused Hetty of not eating. "Kent Cox is so worried about you," she said. "We all are. Such a dear man. I made him come over for a late breakfast and we tried to get him to come picnic with us on Memorial Day, but he can be so shy."

"Hetty knows how shy he is," one of the other women said. "He stayed with you all when Delia left him, didn't he?" When Hetty nodded the woman went on, "He's better off now, but can you imagine living in a theater? Has to be hell to dust. And somebody said his dog pulled down a doily with a candle and set the place on fire last week but it didn't do much damage." The women stayed so long that Hetty finally had to tell them she was getting a headache. She did have a headache by the time they left.

On the last day of July, a Wednesday, at some hour before dawn, Hetty sat up in bed to think about couple of things. One was that she might have to live another thirty or forty or more years without Peter.

The other was that she might as well give up on trying to sleep. She could doze off now and then and she sometimes fell asleep at some hour before dawn but she couldn't actually sleep. She got to thinking about that and decided she had the right to put herself to sleep.

That ought to be anyone's right, she thought. To sleep. To really go to sleep.

Possibly forever.

13

Some mornings Hetty woke up with her face wet, having remembered in her sleep. Sometimes she woke and remembered and it would slam into her all over again and double her over. Hearing herself whimper made her furious.

Being angry helped.

She had to get used to it. This was how she was to swim into wakefulness now, every day, every day for the rest of her life she was to wake up and know. And she would have to work at making herself get out of bed.

Or not.

On Saturday morning, the third day of August, Peg came over and rang Hetty's doorbell half a dozen times and waited and rang it half a dozen times more before Hetty came down to let her in.

Then when Hetty went back upstairs Peg followed her, grunting and lumbering, saying, "Come on, please don't go back to bed, everybody's worried, mostly me." She came puffing into the bedroom to stand over Hetty, making small sad sounds, watching Hetty nestle back beneath the covers.

After a couple of minutes, Peg sat down. "Honey," she said. "Honey. What can I do?"

Hetty said she had a little headache.

Peg rummaged in her overloaded purse and came up with a green and white capsule that looked like something a veterinarian would prescribe for a horse. "Here. This is great stuff. I'll get you some water. No, wait. This is an antihistamine. Let's get in my car, first. I promised the kids I'd bring you home with me."

Hetty said she didn't think she needed an antihistamine and she didn't want to go anywhere.

Peg sat on the bed next to her and started twisting her hair around her fingers. Her hands shook and she spilled some capsules, as she tried to put the capsule back into a small container. They slid into the rumples of the sheets and spread.

Peg went to the linen closet and came back with fresh sheets, saying, falsely jovial, "This room is about as bad as Kevin's."

Hetty suggested she put the sheets down, so Peg sat and looked at her with her eyes sinking into little tan nests of wrinkles. "When did you eat last?" she demanded. When Hetty didn't answer—she couldn't remember—Peg's voice went up. "You don't even look at your palette anymore. When was the last time you picked up a brush? You need to paint, love. You know you do. And Shadow's dish is greasy and empty and his water's growing mosquito larvae." She yanked at her hair. "Know what I ought to do? I ought to take Shadow home with me. Then you'd have to come."

"Take him."

"Oh," Peg said, starting to cry.

"I'm okay," Hetty said. "Honest."

"You're not. You're not," Peg wailed. "I'm not letting you stay here by yourself anymore. So many people love you, don't you know how many people love you? I need you to listen to me. I can't handle this, Hetty, honey, I can't."

"I know," Hetty said. "I'm sorry. Don't keep yanking out your hair." She tried for a smile. "Your head will go shiny in front, like Kent's." She took a breath, thinking. "Your boys need a pet, Peg." Shadow was twining around Peg's ankles. Hetty glanced down and sighed. "See? He loves you. Go ahead and take him. I keep running out of cat food. Kevin and Paul ought to have a pet."

"How can you say that?" Peg demanded.

Hetty got up and went downstairs. She sat down in her kitchen rocker and rocked herself.

Peg came stamping into the kitchen. "I am not letting this happen," Peg said, and started picking up things. When she got to an empty cat chow bag on the floor in front of the pantry she stood with it in her hands, crying.

"Oh, is this something to bawl about? I'm sorry. I came to cheer you up." She tried for a goofy grin but it looked ghastly, with the tears dripping down her face.

"I'm fine," Hetty said.

Peg wiped her eyes, bagged the overflowing trash and took it outside. When she came back, she muttered something about cereal and how there wasn't any milk. She opened a can of tomato soup. "How can you talk about giving up your baby? Shadow loves you."

"Cats don't love people," Hetty said. "They let themselves be loved."

Peg put a bowl of soup on the table. "Here," she said. "Come on. Try."

Hetty swallowed a spoonful of the soup and put the spoon down.

"You want to come with me to go pick up some groceries?" Peg said. "I've got to go to the grocery. You're out of dishwasher soap and we can get fresh fruit. Plums are on sale at H.E.B. and have you seen that whole counter full of all kinds of apples? You like apples." She looked down at Shadow. "We'll pick up cat food and some lovely Stouffer's lasagna, just kidding." Her chin trembled. "A little joke?"

Hetty nodded and smiled. She didn't want to talk any more. "Take Shadow. He probably could do with a change of scenery."

Peg bent to touch the cat with her knuckles and said, choking, "She's trying to get rid of you, Shadow. Do you hear? She's turning into a cat hater, like Louise Gofor and that pimply kid of hers."

"Louise does not hate cats," Hetty said. "She just doesn't like cat hair." She thought for a minute. "But Donald loves Shadow. He'd love to have him."

"Louise says all cats wish people were the size of canaries or mice," Peg said.

Hetty studied her folded hands.

"Oh, why are we discussing who hates cats?" Peg said, her voice going desperate again. "You can't turn into a cat neglecter."

"I'm not," Hetty said. "I'm just tired."

Peg let her head fall into her hands, saying, oh, just what she needed, just what she needed. Shadow walked to her and butted at her ankles with his furry head. "Fine, " Peg said. She got up and went to the front hall closet, got Shadow's carrier and tossed it on the floor in front of Hetty. The carrier bounced and jingled.

Shadow stopped shoving against Peg's ankles, stiffened with indignation and strolled away.

"Kevin's very fond of Shadow," Hetty said. "I should have

given him to you last year when you had to have Butch put down."
Peg held out her arms. "I know you're sick with grief, we all are, all of us, we're all walking wounded. I have to go home." She looked around, slapping at her sides helplessly, looking for her purse, her eyes brimming.

Hetty got up and headed back up the stairs to the peace and quiet of her bedroom, saying, "Take Shadow."

Peg didn't answer. Hetty listened for the door. She didn't hear it shut but after what felt like a long while she heard Peg's car start up and then go down the driveway.

Hetty dozed off and thought she heard Johnny talking to Peter in a woods, demanding to know where he was, the two of them playing hide and seek behind trees.

When she woke, she watched the pattern of sunlight through the leaves at the window and the way a cobweb drifted, in a draft in the corner of the ceiling. She couldn't see any spider, just the drift of web.

When she wearied of watching the web, she got out of bed, went down to the den, sat at Pete's roll-top desk and started to write a note. "All I've ever really done is take care of Pete," she wrote. "So that's all I know." Then she realized that everyone knew that; that there really was no need for a note. Who was she writing a note to? George Gordon? He knew very well how hopeless and useless she was.

She crumpled up the attempt and threw it away.

She went back upstairs, undressed, put the stopper in the bathtub, dumped some Vita-bath under the faucet stream, got out a package of single-edged razor blades and unwrapped one.

As the water rose, foaming, she put the blade on the rim of the tub, climbed in and slid down among the warm scented bubbles. She slapped the inside of her wrist and watched the small blue veins become more visible and felt alongside them next to the bone for the artery.

One of Peter's best students, the girl with scarred wrists who started the poetry club, had once written an essay on how to do this. The essay said that you mustn't sever the artery completely or it would clot. But you shouldn't be too timid or the process would take too long. The trick was to do it with the wrist under water.

Peter had gone to talk with her parents, but he was too late.

Hetty wondered if the girl had cut into the scars on her wrists.

She had the edge of the blade pressed against the inside of her wrist when Shadow began scratching at the bathroom door.

Hetty put the razor blade back on the side of the tub.

Peg must have decided not to take Shadow with her. Hetty wondered if there was any water in his dish.

Now Shadow called from downstairs, in what sounded like the kitchen, wailing, filling the house with sad, yowly, demanding cries.

Great.

That meant that now she would have to get out of the tub and dry off and go downstairs to find something, some tuna or salmon or something and change the water in that dish. It was one thing for a person to want to put herself to sleep and quite another to be the kind of person who let a starving cat walk around and around in a kitchen crying itself to death, parched and starving.

Besides, even wrists held under water would have to hurt, wouldn't they? And someone, probably Peg, would have to come and find her.

It might damage the baby.

Or it might be George Gordon.

Or one of the Gofors. Louise, maybe.

Hetty climbed out of the tub and looked at herself in the steamy mirror, at her tangled wet hair, the dark circles under her bloodshot eyes, her chin, that she seemed to have rubbed almost raw.

After a while she wrapped herself in a towel and tore off some toilet tissue to blow her nose. The toilet tissue was on the roll wrong. She heard a hissing noise and realized she was snickering, standing there staring at a roll of toilet tissue, remembering how Lila Mae made such a federal case of how it always ought to be hung so it would "come readily to the hand, out, not in." Poor old Lila Mae, obsessing about the proper way to load toilet paper. The toilet paper lady, the kids called her.

Pete had grinned about that. "What a way to go down through the generations." But he always looked so sweetly patient anytime anyone came up with "the terlit paper lady." "Lila Mae may be a mite persnickety," he once said, "but that is one lady who is well versed in life's gentle courtesies, isn't she?"

Life's gentle courtesies.

Shadow seemed to have quieted down.

Hetty went to the bedroom and stretched out on the bed, thinking about Peter's slow grin, his laugh, his wonderfully helpless laugh. All kinds of things could trigger it. He'd laugh so hard he'd get to helplessly pawing the air, fighting for breath. How many things they'd laughed at, together.

He'd hate to have her lie around crying. The only thing that brought tears to his eyes was their wanting a baby. And there was poor Peg, so tired of being a mother, so fed up with being pregnant. What wouldn't Peter have given for a little girl or boy. All that money they couldn't afford for specialists and all that timing and hoping and praying and...and nothing. Even that business of how that one big expert had him change to those ridiculous boxer shorts because his Fruit of the Loom briefs were supposed to be too tight and might discourage the sperm count or whatever. He wore those flapping boxer shorts for years, much good they did.

Nothing did any good.

"A cat," Hetty said, aloud. "All we were meant to have is one cat, that someone else threw away." She closed her eyes.

She was dozing when Peg let herself in again and came huffing up the stairs, calling, insistently, "Are you in back in bed again?"

When she reached the bedroom door she said, her voice sounding peculiar, "I think I might be, oof, going into labor."

"Are you serious?"

"Is the Pope Catholic?"

Hetty jumped out of bed and was yanking the zipper of her jeans before Peg could catch her breath. Then, when she said, "Let's go," Peg said to wait a second and stood staring at Hetty with the whites of her eyes gleaming all around the irises, yelling, "Hurry!"

"I am," Hetty said.

"Whoops, whoops," Peg said, lumbering off toward the bathroom. "I'm flooding your carpet. My water just broke."

A minute later she called out something that she and Hetty would laugh at for years, any time they harked back to this moment—

"Ow, ow, *ow!* This is it. I'm having a baby. Hey: what'll you give me to not tell Lila Mae you got your toilet paper on wrong?"

14

A New Life

Hetty drove, faster than she ever had, with Peg panting, saying, "Oh, hurry, oh, be careful, oh, be careful, but please could you hurry? oh, oh, oooh," so that Hetty's hands slid around on the steering wheel all the way up Fuqua and down Beamer Boulevard.

The woman at the desk in the admitting room took one look at Peg going, "whoo whoo whoo," her face gleaming with perspiration, and the next thing Hetty knew a man came flying through a pair of swinging doors with a gurney. Peg was loaded up and wheeled away.

Hetty found a telephone in an alcove and called Peg's mother. Leona didn't seem to realize what a glorious thing Peg was doing.

"This is it," Hetty said. "Now. Right this minute. She's having the baby."

Leona said it was about time.

"We're at the hospital," Hetty said.

"So one would assume," Peg's mother said.

After a time, Hetty was allowed in the room with Peg. Peg held her hands and panted and pulled. Hard. When she relaxed between efforts, she grimaced and grinned and licked her upper lip. "Love you," she said. "God. Thanks. Don't cry. I love you better than any adult person I know."

"Me, too. Me, too," Hetty said. "This is so glorious, oh, it is. Oh, Peg."

"Glad you're having such a great time," Peg said. "Whoo. Whoo. Don't cry."

Hetty couldn't stop crying, even when she was sent out to pace in the hall. It was all so wonderfully exciting, so splendid, such a grand *important* thing Peg was doing. And she had a share in it.

She could hear Peter, his smiling voice: "They also serve who only stand and wait."

The aqua tinted waiting room outside labor and delivery felt very different from that wretched room outside the intensive care unit. The magazines on the glass-topped table had laughing babies on every single cover. Hetty leafed through a couple of them, giddy with ecstasy and fatigue, promising herself that no one, no one, not even Peg, would ever know about how a person could sit around fiddling with a stupid razor blade in a bathtub.

How cold Peg's mom's voice had sounded, on the phone. Still so disapproving. So scornful. Like Louise, that time when Hetty had made the mistake of saying "the miracle of birth."

"What's miraculous about it?" Louise had demanded. "A miracle would be a fish or a tree, not another baby. Look at all the low rent people. Pop pop, popping out babies like popcorn."

Louise and Dave hadn't even been terribly happy about Donald, when he was born. Dave kept saying baby Donald looked like a skinned rabbit. Well, he did, poor thing. What a long night that was. But what a sweet little boy Donny turned out to be, for the longest time. Such a serious child, even as a toddler. Little Donny walked around with the weight of the world on his bowed shoulders from the time he learned to walk. Not a bit like his sturdy sister. Doris always had those hard, apple-shiny cheeks. Her fat little sausage fingers kept curling into fists, all the way through school. Gracious. Was it Louise or David or his sullen big sister that turned that please-love-me little boy into such a timorous teenager?

When had Donald lost that sweet smile? During adolescence? Yes. It had to have been about the time he'd learned how to drive. The spring when he had started to have such awful complexion problems. Well, no wonder. He'd spent evening after evening of his fifteenth year underneath that old truck in the driveway across the street and he never did get to drive the thing. David took it up to the lake house or some place.

The Gofor family had argued endlessly about buying that truck. Louise wanted a Mazda and David had insisted the Mazda pickup in that model was exactly like the Ford pickup. "You can't tell 'em apart." Louise finally had backed down when he took her to the dealership and showed her, but she never much cared for driving a truck. Simply didn't fancy herself the pickup truck type.

Hetty got up, stretched and looked at her watch. Almost eight-thirty.

Leona brought Paul and Kevin into the waiting room a little after 8:40, just before Peg's third son came into the world at two minutes to nine.

The baby weighed nine pounds and seven ounces. "Huge," Leona said. "Absolutely huge."

"That's right, Mom," Peg said. "It was all that junk food." Then she looked at Hetty and her voice softened. "I'm naming him Edward. That means 'a guard' and that's what this kid looks like, doesn't he? Like all the guys in our crowd. Bunch of big brutes. I just knew this baby would have shoulders like Jerome's. And look at all that Indian hair and the mad Albright glint in his eye."

Leona sniffed.

"Looks sort of like Dustin Hoffman, in a way," Peg said, dreamily. "Don't you think?"

"No," Leona said.

"No," Hetty said. "You must be delirious."

The nurses didn't think Edward looked like Dustin Hoffman either. As soon as they suggested that Leona and Hetty and the boys let Peg get some rest Leona was in a hurry to leave but Hetty and Paul and Kevin wanted to go stand outside the glassed-in wall of the newborn nursery. "We want to see the baby," Hetty told her. "I'll deliver the kids, after a bit."

The nurses had the newborns in rows of baskets lined with soft curls of wool, like cherubim on clouds. Edward, pink and lusty, had a full head of black feathery hair and a triple chin. "He's the biggest baby in there," Paul said. "But, gee. He's little, isn't he?"

"Oh, he is," Hetty said. "Mister Bach and I came to see you when you were born. We stood right here looking and looking at you when you were this little, just like this."

"Me, too?" Kevin asked.

"You, too, when you came along," Hetty said, touching his cheek with the backs of her fingers.

"How come you and Mister Bach never had a baby?" Kevin asked.

"Oh, we'd have loved to," Hetty said. "But Peg has been pretty generous with you, you know. She shares. And the Schmulbecks let us baby-sit Emily. What a darling baby she was. She stayed bald for the longest time and then there was all this lovely, red, gold, curly hair. Emily has the loveliest coloring, hasn't she? Like her mother. She had to wear the glasses, of course, early on. Made her look so studious. Such a busy little person, even as a toddler. Once we left Mister Bach with her when Emily was about four and Hallie and I came back to find him bumping around under the dining room table because little Emily insisted he had to be a good doggy and wouldn't let him come out from under there."

Kevin grinned. "That sounds like Emily. My dad says she's spoiled."

"Oh, I don't know as that's true," Hetty said. "Maybe when she was little, she might have been a little headstrong. She was so cute, so studious and solemn. She used to climb up on Peter's knee and he'd just melt. Just shake his head and melt."

"Emily Schmulbeck," Paul said. "Huh." He gave Hetty a knowing sideways look. "She goes with the Dutchman. Don't tell her dad. He won't even let her go to a movie with anybody or go to a school dance or anything else and she's, like, seventeen."

"I'm not sure that's anyone's business but Emily's," Hetty said.

"This guy, he's got this motorcycle—" Paul said but Kevin interrupted him.

"Look at how the baby scrunches up his mouth," he said, imitating. "Did I used to do that?"

"Emily's dad would, like, die all over the place," Paul went on. "He'd probably kill her and the Dutchman both. No kidding."

Kevin jostled his brother. "Who cares?" He touched Hetty's arm. "What was it like when we were born?" He sighed happily. "Were you born here, too?"

"Oh, no," Hetty said. "I was born in a house." Both boys looked at her. "A big old Victorian house in Galveston," she said. "It's a frat house now, where a lot of boys live. But when we lived there my dad used to call it the House of The Lord. That was our name, remember. You know my dad. George Gordon Lord."

"My dad says he's a hot dog," Kevin said. He thought of something else. "How come you to not have a baby?" he asked again.

Paul glanced at Hetty and gave his brother a shove. "You already asked that."

"That's okay," Hetty said. "I didn't answer, did I, Kev?" She put her hand on Kevin's head; his pale hair was as fine and soft as Peg's. "I guess having a baby isn't something everybody can do."

"Some people only have one," Kevin said. "One baby. That's what my grandmother says." He thought about that. "Were you the only little kid in your house?" He twisted away from Paul. "Quit." He moved closer to Hetty. "How come you to live in a frat house?" He closed his eyes and opened them and said, unhappily. "My mom thinks our house is too big, now."

"I know," Hetty said. "My father won the down payment for our Galveston house by playing Liar's Poker at a club called the Saints and Sinners," she said. "Now, what do you think of that?"

"What's Liar's Poker?" Kevin had to know.

"She just said." Paul looked derisive. "It's a game, stupid. Go on," he told Hetty.

"Well, my daddy won the pot in this poker game and he proposed to my mother on the steps of our house. My mother always used to say that she said she'd marry him because she was about half afraid the railing he had her backed up against would cave in and she'd fall into the shrubbery."

"If it's a frat house it must be pretty big," Paul said.

"It looks rather grand," Hetty said. "But that house was a tad saggy at the seams when we lived there. The wiring was dangerous and the plumbing could be tricky. But those old houses are wonders in a storm. They're made of Cypress, you know. They rock and creak and sail through hurricanes the way old sailing ships used to weather heavy seas." She waved her hands and swayed, slightly, demonstrating.

"You live through any storms?"

"That we did," Hetty said.

"Bet you had some kind of a Christmas tree," Kevin said.

"What's that got to do with anything?" Paul asked. "Who's talking about Christmas?" He looked at Hetty and shrugged. "He does that."

"We had some dandy Christmases," Hetty said. "And some not so dandy. My mother had quite a temper."

The Field

"And now she's married to somebody else," Paul said. "Your mom went away. Sort of like my dad. Look at the baby's thumb," he said. "It's flat. How did it get so flat? That little bugger must have been sucking his thumb all this time, in there."

He was right. Both the baby's thumbs were flattened. His small translucent fingers had nails so shiny they looked polished. He kept flexing his hands, making groping motions as the boys and Hetty gazed in companionable silence.

After Kevin went off to find a men's room, Paul's eyes stayed on the baby but he started to talk, without any inflection. "You want to know something? My dad says he might get married again as soon as he can," he confided in a croak. "He says he might not have a choice."

His brow was against the glass. "He probably got his girlfriend knocked up."

Hetty knew better than to touch him until he leaned against her.

As soon as he did, she let herself give him a brief, fierce hug.

He pulled away and ran his hand through his hair before he went on. "Kind of hard to know what my dad means. He says he can't let her down. Pamela." He sighed and went on, gazing straight ahead, focusing on the baby. "Like, Pamela? We saw her, dad and me and Kevin, once, a long time ago and she acted like they knew each other real well. Kev didn't snap but I did. Dad took us to see 'Old Yeller,' the twilight show at Almeda? and there was this line waiting to get in. Kev kept fussing about how long it took, the line and all, and this woman turned around and looked at dad and he looked at her and they had these little sneaky smiles."

"Kev didn't get it. But I did. I got it, right away.

"Later on, in the lobby, next to the drinking fountain? Dad said he was going to the john and I kept waiting and then I came out and they were standing there talking with my dad's hand on her butt. Like it was just normal, you know."

He made a small sad snorting sound that he tried to turn into a laugh.

"They went somewhere and told us to go on back and see the movie. So we did. Kev and me saw 'Old Yeller' two and a half times and the manager had to bring us into his office so he could call up our house so he could close up. That's how long it took my dad to come back and get us."

He looked at Hetty. "So now it turns out he can't let her down. Pamela. He can't let her down again." He shrugged and looked away.

Kevin was coming back along the corridor, dawdling, deliberately scuffing the side of one of his shoes along the baseboard at the side of the carpet. There was just time for Hetty to startle Paul with another quick hug. When she let him go she didn't trust herself to say anything.

In the car, on the way to Leona's, Kevin asked, "You think we ought to call Dad about the baby?" and Paul said, in his croaky voice, "Naw."

After she'd dropped off the boys, Hetty was suddenly so tired it was an effort to think, to make herself stop in at Kroger's, to pick up a bag of kitty litter and cat food and tomato juice and milk.

She wrestled with the new lock on the back door for several minutes and finally had to put the groceries down and carefully insert the key and lean on the door to get it to open. Shadow's going to be furious, she thought, as she came into the kitchen. His dish is licked clean.

He was hiding. The kitchen clock said nearly midnight but Hetty went walking all through the house calling, meowing cat noises, too tired, really, for games but she felt so guilty. She checked all the places Shadow could get into; the hinged door to the laundry room, the downstairs bathroom, the pantry, the corner under the bottom shelf of the linen closet, even the area beneath her painting table, though he never went there.

Her painting area was a mess. She hadn't been near her table or palettes since Memorial Day. The paints were dried and cracked in the wells of the palettes. She'd have to get rid of them and start fresh. The table was filmed with dust. No cat prints on it. She stood gazing, for a long moment, at her papers and brushes, at the lovely, thick, textured pastels and bits of fabric she had been so excited about. Before. In that other life. Some of her brushes hung in their holder, as enticing as any cat toys but Shadow never touched them. He knew better.

Poor baby.

The Field

He wasn't under any of the beds.

Finally she gave up and went back to the kitchen, announcing, with a prodigious yawn, "Well, *be* that way. See who cares."

She upended tuna into the cat dish, made some final conciliatory clucking noises and headed back up the stairs.

She hesitated at the hall window at the top of the stairs, noticing the play of moonlight across her zinnias out in front and the look of Louise Gofor's pansies and ivy in the beds alongside the sidewalk, across the street.

The lights of an oncoming car swept across the street, illuminating a broken box, or something, some sort of trash left out in the middle of the pavement. The car swerved, evidently trying to avoid hitting whatever it was.

Another car came around the corner and hit the thing.

It took Hetty a couple of seconds to realize that the thing bouncing around on the concrete down there was Shadow's carrying case.

She leaped down the carpeted stair, skidded past several steps, ran, sobbing, into the front hall, got the front door unlocked and jerked it open in time to see another vehicle, a truck, this time, run over the case.

It was Shadow's carrying case.

What was left of it.

It wasn't empty. As she watched, the carrier hit the far curb and bounced, rattling, into the gutter.

*

Hetty ran out, grabbed up the broken box and collapsed on the curb with it in her arms.

She couldn't seem to let go of it. She was still hugging it to her breast, hurting her arms on jagged edges of broken plastic and tangled wire, when Lieut. Gray drove up. He swerved to the curb, parked and got out of his car. He got to her before she could get to her feet, saying, "Let me take that." He eased the carrier from her and walked up the walk with it.

After he'd put it down next to the front door, he came back and held out a hand. Hetty gripped his hand and arm and let herself be led into the house. She walked through the house to the kitchen and sat down in her rocker and held herself, rocking, while he brought the carrier in and took it through the kitchen door. "We'll get to this in a couple of minutes," he said.

Hetty started to answer and sobbed.

She couldn't stop crying.

The lieutenant let her cry. He walked around the room, looking at the windows and the walls and the floor, stopping to gaze at the painting across from the biggest window. It was hanging slightly crooked. He reached up and straightened it.

After a couple of minutes Hetty looked over at him and saw that he was getting out his handkerchief and his eyes were closed. The man was blinking away tears. Silently. "Oh, I'm so sorry," she said, "I'm making such awful noises I'm scaring myself. I'll be all right. Truly."

He blew his nose and wiped his eyes and went and opened the drawer next to the sink, got out a cup towel, dampened it under the faucet and came back and handed it to her. He paced back and forth and came to stand in front of her with his hands clasped, not watching her wipe her eyes.

"How can I help?" he said.

"Well, to start with, don't cry," Hetty told him.

He held out his hands, palms up, a helpless gesture. She stood up and let herself be held, briefly, in an enveloping hug. His shirt had a clean smooth feel and the comforting scent of soap and aftershave.

But he was a stranger, she realized. A pitying stranger. In her kitchen. Her untidy kitchen. She drew away. "Thank you. I'll be fine. "Do you have time for a cup of tea?"

He nodded.

"Do you drink tea?"

"Sometimes."

Hetty forgot how tired she was, then, in her need to talk. The lieutenant didn't write anything down but she had the feeling that he heard, truly heard and recorded, somewhere in himself, every nuance of every word. When she told him how Peter had found Shadow, a little scrap of a thing, abandoned, on a freeway esplanade, he looked at her with his upper lip caught beneath his teeth, shaking his head. She hadn't felt such quiet sympathy, such empathy, in months. "He came in the door with this tiny starveling in his pocket, like that Norman Rockwell illustration, " Hetty said, her voice breaking. "Actually in his rain coat pocket. Shadow was about this big." She cupped her hands. "One of the neighbors suggested we name the poor little thing 'Road Kill.'"

"Would that be the neighbor across the street?"

"David Gofor," Hetty said. "Yes. He thought he was being funny." She sipped her tea. "David's a good person, he's very generous and he can be clever. He just sounds so gruff because he feels, I don't know. Inadequate? His dad sounded like that, too. That's such an unhappy house. Donny is going to be sick about Shadow. He and Doris have never had a pet of their own. Louise thinks it's disgusting to keep animals in the house."

"That so?"

"Oh," Hetty said. "I wouldn't want you to think David or Louise could possibly hurt an animal. I'm just nattering. I don't know anyone who could hurt an animal."

"Of course not," the lieutenant said.

"I don't want to sit around trying to think who could do this to Shadow," Hetty said. "I don't want to see such a person, see how they are, see the world through their terrible eyes. Am I sounding crazy? I am crazy. I'm just sick. Such a person would have to be sick with grief, right now, too. Scratching and gouging at himself. Suffering. Sick."

"It's a sickening thing," he said. "Yes."

"You're probably going to be practical," she said. "Look for a car with scratches on it or some such thing. Well, don't tell me if you find one. I don't want to know. Especially if it's some youngster. I can't bear it."

"Do you think it was some youngster?"

"I don't know," she said. "I can't stand it. Somebody damaged. A lost soul."

"There are people without feeling," he said. "It happens."

"Then they're really lost souls. Hopelessly, horribly lost."

She didn't want to cry anymore. "I don't know what to do, now," she said. "What am I to do? What do people do? You must see a lot of people who feel this way. Don't look like that, please. I'm not asking for sympathy. I'm drowning in sympathy. Sympathy doesn't help a person get through the tunnel."

She studied the knuckles of her hands. "Do you know what I

mean? It's very dark. The tunnel."

He nodded.

"People keep reminding me how long it's been," she said. "As if that has anything to do with anything. Peter is gone. He's gone. How many months he's been gone has nothing to do with it. He's gone, now. Tomorrow, when I wake up, he'll still be gone."

She stood up and walked around the kitchen and came back. "I'm not going to think about that right now."

The window over the sink was a black rectangle. She went over to it and drew the blinds. She put Shadow's dishes in the sink and ran water over them and loaded them into the dishwasher. Some of the dishes in the sink had dried food in them. When she threw the placemat that had been under the dishes into the trash she could hardly get the lid closed. "I'm afraid this place is a mess." She turned to look at the detective. He was standing in front of her painting, seemingly deeply engrossed.

"Did you do this?" he said.

"Yes."

"It's beautiful. These rocks and the water." He shook his head. "The colors in the reflections. I can't see how you did it."

"It's a collage," she said. "It's pretty simple." She didn't care to discuss it. She wiped her hands. "If you can write your name you can be taught to paint."

She looked at her watch. "Oh, dear. I'm afraid it's very late. I'm going to have to let you go. I'm going to have a small funeral and tuck in for the night. I'll be all right. Gracious. I didn't mean to keep you here so very late. You'll have to forgive me."

He said, hesitantly, his voice so gentle that she wasn't sure what he was saying until he repeated himself, "I'm quite capable with a spade."

Hetty fought a rush of gratitude.

"We'll need a shroud." She fetched one of Peter's Hawaiian shirts from the stack of clean paint rags in the bottom of the linen closet so the lieutenant could wrap Shadow in it. She stood by, watching him fold the fabric's blue sky and red hibiscus blossoms and splashy leaves into a neatly swaddled bundle.

He insisted on doing the digging. She held the flashlight. After he covered the grave and mounded it, they stood out in the back yard, in quiet companionship, until Hetty yawned and said, "I'm so cried out I'm almost giddy. You've been a tremendous help. It feels right, somehow, that we used that particular shirt. Peter wore that thing until the seams frayed and I confiscated it, but I never could bring myself to turn it into a paint rag and stain it every which way. Now it's a winding cloth, for heaven's sake."

"For heaven's sake," the lieutenant said.

While he was washing his hands at the spigot in the back yard, the lieutenant asked Hetty if she would very much mind calling him Tom. "Not all the time, of course. Just when you're comfortable with it," he said, diffidently. He straightened up and frowned and, as he looked at her, smiled anxiously through the creases bracketing his eyes. "Just, you know. When we're having a cup of tea?"

"Or a funeral," Hetty said.

"Oh, there's a sad smile," he said.

"As is yours," Hetty answered. "As is yours, Tom." She lifted her chin. "Well. Thank you, sir. Maybe Peter thanks you."

"I'd like to think so," he said.

"He had a variety of ways of thanking people." She thought for a moment. "I am grateful beyond decent expression."

The lieutenant doffed an imaginary cap. "One is glad of the opportunity." He looked away. "Would I be giving advice if I suggest that you try to get some rest? I'm going to park out in front for a while."

"Couldn't you use some rest?" Hetty asked.

He smiled. "I'm on duty," he said.

It was a comfort, knowing he was out there. Watching. And thinking. Truly paying attention.

I'm going to go see Peg and baby Edward tomorrow morning, Hetty told herself. This morning. I am going to visit that wonderful baby this morning. Think of that.

She fell asleep and dreamed she was cleaning the kitchen so Baby Edward could play on a blanket on the floor with Shadow. And Johnny Schmulbeck was there, in the dream, up near the corner of the ceiling. Johnny was floating, looking very sad, with Kent looking over his shoulder, arguing.

16

Hetty didn't get to the hospital until after four o'clock on Monday afternoon. She found Peg sitting up, pale and tranquilly languishing, haloed in a shaft of sunlight, in a quilted bed jacket with a matching blue ribbon holding her hair back and little Edward cradled in her arms.

"I brought some See's chocolates for the nurses," Hetty said, "and some fruit for you. Who gave you the bed jacket? It's perfect."

"Thanks." Peg looked down at herself and her mouth curled into a smile. "Kind of shiny, isn't it?

"The boys brought it. I suspect they used up every nickel of Paul's embryonic coin collection on it. He'll probably be sorry, but right now he's carried away with all this." The jacket, of machine quilted rayon satin, had a K-Mart label poking up at the back of Peg's neck.

Hetty tucked it in. "Well, I think you look lovely in it."

The jacket had come, Peg said, in a slightly used box, with quantities of tissue, with the blue satin ribbon she had in her hair tied around it.

"You look like a Madonna," Hetty said, slightly awed at this dimpled beatific Peg, with her sleepy, rosy, little baby at her breast.

"Oh?" Peg grinned.

"I mean lovely," Hetty said. "Almost holy."

"Goes with the territory," Peg said, musing. She stroked the baby's downy head with the back of a finger.

"Donald Gofor came over for a little bit," Hetty said.

Peg grimaced. "You didn't give him a key to the new locks, did you? I know how fond of him you are but, gee. He's a teenager, after all. What did he want?"

The Field

"To offer his condolences."

Peg looked quizzical. "Again?"

Hetty waited until the nurse had taken the baby away before she said, "More condolences. For...for something that happened last night," and told Peg about Shadow.

She wished she hadn't. She thought she was all cried out but when Peg said, "Aw," she burst into tears and Peg cried with her. Peg made enough noise for both of them.

After they calmed down, Peg said, "We don't know anyone who would kill Shadow. I should have taken him." She sighed. "How did they get in? It had to be those bikers. Didn't you say once that you thought Clifford what's his name could get into any house, any time? It had to have been him. I saw him cart off Emily after the funeral on the back of his--"

"I'm not at all sure we locked the door," Hetty said. "We were in a bit of a hurry, remember? When I finally got home, I fiddled with the key for what felt like forever, locking and unlocking the kitchen door."

"So your Bandido friend walked in," Peg said.

"Clifford Van Huys. And no. He didn't," Hetty said.

"Because?"

"Because he is a friend. Because Peter tutored him. I told you about that. And because Lieutenant Gray says Clifford and his gang were in San Antonio on Memorial Day weekend. And mostly because Clifford would not hurt Shadow. I know he wouldn't."

"Well, I guess we don't know anything, then," Peg said. She sighed. "Back to the drawing board."

"But we might somehow know something," Hetty said. "Minds are wonderfully strange, Peg. People don't think in an orderly way, straight along. Especially when it comes to remembering. Memories come in clusters and bunches, like grapes." She paused and took a deep breath and made herself go on. "What if it was one of us? What if—oh, don't look like that—what if one of the boys, a friend, someone decent and good, who never would want to injure anyone, somehow lost all control for that just that one single moment and—"

Peg sat up, her eyes sharp. "Quit. What are you saying?"

"I don't know. I don't know," Hetty said. "But what if Kent

lost his temper and flailed out and socked Peter? He did once before, remember? When he was drinking and Pete took away his car keys?"

"Oh, that was flailing around," Peg said.

"Peter had to have a dentist check his teeth the next day," Hetty said.

Peg's tugged at her hair. "You never told me that."

Hetty shrugged. "Kent didn't mean it. He'd never mean to loosen anyone's teeth, but, oh, Peg, what if it was a hideous accident? It's only in the movies or on TV that men hit men with their fists and the men they've hit get up and brush themselves off and walk away."

"I know." Peg looked as if she were trying to be deliberately calming.

"Yes. All right," Hetty said. "Let's think about that. How do you think that person, maybe not Kent, but anyone. How would he be feeling?"

"Like telling the police that he didn't mean to do it," Peg said. "That's how he'd be feeling. You're making me crazy."

"But he wouldn't necessarily feel like telling anyone. He might be too scared. And ashamed. And guilty. He'd just want it to go away. I don't know," Hetty said.

"No, you don't."

Hetty couldn't stop. "It seems impossible that David or Johnny or Kent could hurt Peter and leave him like that, but the detectives are investigating all of them, all Peter's friends." She paused. Her voice dropped. "And mine. My friends. Our dearest, oldest friends who have been our friends forever. Kent, for instance."

Peg looked as though she might burst into tears again. She seemed relieved when a nurse hurried in with the baby, saying he was hungry.

"This one stays hungry," the nurse said.

"I know," Peg said.

It was impossible to talk about any sort of tragedy with Peg feeding her hungry son. After he'd nursed, Edward yawned hugely.

Peg looked down at him, smiling. "Isn't he tremendous? Remember how tiny Emily was? Born the day before Christmas. And Doris. Remember what a big fat baby Louise's Doris was? Over ten and a half pounds. And David going around acting disappointed because he wanted a boy. Somebody should have smacked him alongside the head. And then they had this skinny little Donald. And there's David, disappointed again, because the kid looked like a skinned rabbit. Skinniest baby any of us ever saw. Spent the first couple of months of his life in an incubator and he's been a walking nervous breakdown ever since."

"He is not," Hetty said. "But poor Emily. Born on the day before Christmas. Peter once offered to give her his birthday and let her take his, so she could have a better birthday."

"Sounds like Peter," Peg said. "But Emily was Johnny's little Christmas present and he's been trying to keep her wrapped up ever since. I wonder how he feels about her going off with Clifford."

"Johnny is suffering so, Peg," Hetty said. "He loved Peter dearly."

"Oh, I know," Peg said. "Everybody knows about suffering Johnny. First he was dying all over the place over the empty nest thing and then, then we all have this end of the world." She thought for a minute. "I don't get the empty nest syndrome. A lot of men have such a terrible time with having the kids leave but shoot—" Her grin went lopsided—"when I finally ship my kids off, I'll pop champagne corks all over the place and call in the neighbors. But Johnny and Hallie are falling all apart and Emily's not even left for school yet."

Hetty said, "You'd think they'd approve of Sweetsue. She does seem awfully young, though."

"Hallie." Peg put her finger down her throat, feigning a retch. "The total wife and mother. Of course, that is what men want, isn't it? That's what they all want, these sweet, little, pretty, little—"

"Don't," Hetty said.

"I'm not, but it *is*, isn't it?" The satin ribbon in Peg's hair had slipped. She yanked it off, tucked her hair back behind her ears and stuck her chin out. "Oh, yeah, that's what they want. And the younger and skinnier, the better."

"Emily's an excellent student," Hetty said, changing the subject. "Peter was so pleased with her. 'Johnny worries too much,' he said, 'but that young lady is the lass with the delicate air.' She won an award with a poem."

Peg looked at the ceiling. "Oh, terrific. Poetry. Like her daddy. Now that'll set her up for this world, won't it?" She hesitated. "At least it's better than if she were riding off into the sunset on the back of somebody's Harley...or something." She closed her mouth and looked away.

A nurse came and gathered up the baby, and Peg settled back into the bed in a way that made Hetty realize it must be time to go.

*

The next night Hetty drove Peg and the baby home to a very clean house and a starchy clean Leona, who said she was at her wit's very end with trying to get Paul and Kevin to eat anything other than macaroni and cheese and hot dogs, which had to be so bad for them. Hetty felt as though she were abandoning Peg to her own mother in her own house.

*

Two weeks later, on the fifteenth, a Wednesday night, Lieutenant Tom Gray called Hetty. He said he was at home. He said he wanted to check in with her to see if she was all right, from time to time, if that was all right with her.

Hetty thanked him.

Then he asked her whether she'd begun to remember anything more that he and Lieutenant Stephens ought to know.

Hetty said she hadn't anything more to tell him.

There was a longish pause and when he said something more Hetty missed it but she could hear stringed instruments tuning behind his voice. At first she thought the sound of the strings might be a radio but an interruption in the thready tuning call of a violin and the plaintive response of a viola made her realize that there must be musicians getting ready to play somewhere nearby.

She asked, "Are you having a recital?"

The lieutenant sounded even more hushed than usual. "Got some friends who come by of a Wednesday."

"Lovely," Hetty said. "What do you play?"

"Cello," he said. He was silent for a moment.

He asked, again, if she was all right.

She said she was.

What had happened to Shadow was dreadful, he said.

She said it certainly was.

The Field

He wanted to offer his sympathy. Again. He'd once had a cat.

"For a good many years. A Siamese. They talk, you know. Go around sounding off. This darned thing used to walk around mouthing off all the time. Hardly ever shut up."

He laughed quietly. "Can't tell you how much I miss her."

Then his voice changed. He wondered how well Hetty might know Clifford Van Huys.

"He's a student," Hetty told him. "One of the ones Peter tutored."

"A little slow?"

"Not at all," Hetty said. "No. I think Peter found him to be very bright. He just needed a bit of a boost. He's given us every evidence of being most grateful for it, too. He once sent me a box of Godiva chocolates."

"A mannerly young man," the lieutenant said. He cleared his throat. "Godiva. Well, well."

The strings were warming up more strenuously.

He raised his voice. "But Mr. Van Huys has been a student for a few years."

"Yes," Hetty said.

"He, ah, he seems to be taking an interest in a lot of things that he might better leave alone. You might want to use whatever influence you have to get him to stand clear of our investigation."

"Stand clear?" Hetty was puzzled. "Of...of the investigation?"

"Right," the lieutenant said. "I won't say he's obstructing justice but the young man would seem to be taking an interest and there's a fine line there, that we don't want him stumbling across, now do we?"

"We?" Hetty said. "What in the world are you saying?"

"I'm saying if you have anything to do with young Van Huys' getting in the way of our investigation it might be a good idea to call him off."

"I wouldn't begin to know how to call anyone off," Hetty said, trying for hauteur. "I haven't talked to Clifford in years. I thought he was no longer a suspect."

"Is Mr. Van Huys in your driveway?"

"Of course not." Hetty ran to the window in the kitchen. "There's no one in my driveway."

"Good," the lieutenant said. "Do you like chamber music?"

"What? What?" Hetty said. "Chamber music? Yes, of course. But what was all that about Clifford Van Huys?"

"I think you know."

"Just a minute, here," Hetty said.

"Oh, just a minute, I'm concerned," the lieutenant said.

"Really," Hetty said.

"Really. Yes. Concerned. Worried. About you," the lieutenant said. "That's it. Van Huys may be a big fan of your husband and he may send chocolates, but the guy's dangerous. He's a biker. A gangster."

"Good evening," Hetty said.

"Ah, wait," Tom said. "I just called to see if you're—to warn you—but I didn't want to scare you—"

"I'm not at all frightened," Hetty said. "Have you been drinking? I'm not accustomed to listening to gentlemen who have been drinking. Good night."

"But I haven't," Tom said. "Well, yes. Not a great deal. I mean, it's not a problem. Look, I'm holding up the works, here. I'm going to have to let you go." He added, hastily, almost growling, "Do you have tickets to the symphony? We have the best symphony in the world."

"I know," Hetty said, in some confusion. "Go play your cello."

"Yes," he said. "Goodbye." She said goodbye but neither of them hung up.

"It's good that you have at least one night a week for your music," Hetty said.

"Ah, but I don't always," Tom said. "We had five homicides on one of my supposed days off. Five. In one twenty-four hour period."

Hetty suddenly realized that his voice was very like the sound of a cello. A chocolatey voice. D-minor. His phrasing blended in with the low cry of a viola.

"This is a dangerous town," he was saying. "You mustn't try to do what we are paid to do. Van Huys is a biker. I am told he and his buddies are trying to help you figure out what happened to Mister Bach. I hope you aren't involved in anything crazy. But you wouldn't be."

The Field

Hetty said she had no idea what he was talking about. "You"ve been drinking?"

"A couple of beers," Tom said. "That's all I ever have. My friends, here, are waiting for me. Now, then. Good. Good. We've got all that settled. You're going to leave the driving to us, right?"

After a moment he added, so softly that Hetty had to cover the mouthpiece of the telephone and strain at listening to hear him, "And don't be giving away a lot of keys to your house, please, Mrs. Bach, ma'am."

She said she wouldn't.

"Thing is," he said. "We seem to be getting a lot of volunteer help. Helpful volunteers can make things difficult, for themselves and for us. It's a mess."

Hetty told him she didn't understand. She truly didn't.

Tom said, "Call if you think of anything at all that you want to talk about. Will you do that?"

He had, she decided, sounded ever so slightly drunk. And no wonder, with such a dreadful job. He'd sounded plaintive. And nice. Tickets to the symphony, indeed.

17

Donald Gofor

On Monday afternoon Donald's mother came up with this terrific idea: she wanted Donald to go with her to the pet store in the mall so they could buy a nice little kitty for him to take across the street to Hetty.

It took Donald about an hour, him and his dad both, to talk her out of it. And she still wouldn't give it a rest. "A cat is a cat," she said. "Well, I'll pick up some brownies at Randall's and you can take them over there, then. Hetty dotes on you. Maybe she'll give you one of her new keys. We've always had a key to the Bach's. Always. It just slays me that she had that Jerome Albright change all the locks. She trusts that sleazy husband of Peg's more than those of us who've been right here for her, for forever."

Hetty was out in back, spreading mulch in the flower bed along the fence. She looked up and smiled at Donald and said, "Well, hi, there." She looked kind of pale and her eyelids were swollen some but she didn't seem as sick as she had been. She asked Donald if he could use a Coke because she sure could use a break and rinsed off her hands at the outside spigot. "Just loosening up some dirt out here," she said. "How are you doing?"

Donald said he was fine and followed her into the kitchen. She got out a Coke for him. When she took an ice cube tray out of the refrigerator and started to wrestle with it, Donald said, "Let me do that," and she smiled like she used to, for a minute.

She put a filter in the top of the coffee maker and measured coffee beans into the grinder. While the grinder was doing its thing the phone rang. Hetty stopped the grinder and answered it and said, smiling past the phone at Donald, that she had a visitor. "Why

The Field

don't I call you back?"

But then she added, "Why, thank you, Kent," and Donald got a chill. Before she hung up, she said, "That would be lovely."

No, it wouldn't, Donald thought.

The morning paper was on the table, still in its plastic sleeve. Donald pulled it out and said, casually, looking at the funnies which he'd already seen, "You might want to be careful of Mr. Cox. He's got some loose pickets in his fence."

"Kent?" Hetty looked disapproving. "Mr. Cox is just trying to be kind. Everybody is."

Not everybody, Donald thought. But what he said was, "Oh, there I go, messing up."

Hetty made a little face, forgiving him, and Donald started over. "He's not the greatest guy in the world or anything," he said.

Hetty got a couple of napkins out of a drawer. "He's been through a lot."

"Yeah, well, he puts other people through a lot," Donald said.

She sat down across from him. "Is that so?"

"When he was a little kid he chopped through a turtle's shell once, with a Boy Scout hatchet," Donald said. "You believe that?"

She didn't look like she did.

"Well," Donald said. "I'm not making it up."

"I see," she said.

"Everybody knows about it."

Hetty folded and unfolded her napkin. "Donald," she said, "you have a wonderful imagination. It's such a good thing to have."

"A lot of guys know about it," Donald said. "No kidding."

"There used to be an expression," Hetty said, after a minute. "It's one of my dad's. If someone said something awful about someone to my dad, he'd ask, 'Vas you dere, Charley?'"

Donald thought about that. "Well," he said. "I see your point. But he's got a helluva temper, the Cocksman. Some kids have dropped shop because of it."

Hetty frowned and looked at her hands. "And where did that dreadful name come from? 'The Cocksman.'" She frowned like something smelled bad. "If Kent is something of a ladies' man I guess that's his business. He's been alone long enough."

Donald shrugged. "My mom and dad think he's crazy in love

with you. That's what everybody calls him. The Cocksman.

"You want to know something? You know how he's been saying that he was up at the lake on Memorial Day? Well, that happens to be a lie. Bill Chaney and me saw him driving this snow-cone truck over on Telephone Road on Memorial Day. We told the cops, too. When they were over at the house. They said they'd look into it."

"A snow-cone truck?" Hetty looked puzzled. "Kent Cox?"

"That's what he does, like in the summer or on holidays or after school? He used to pump gas but now he sells snow cones but he don't want anybody to know."

"Doesn't," Hetty said, absently.

"Doesn't want anybody to know," he said. "But we do."

He didn't seem to be getting anywhere much with her. He figured it might be time to change the subject. He swallowed some of his Coke and swallowed a belch and looked around. He didn't mean to sit and stare at the place in front of a cabinet where Shadow's dish used to be but that's where he ended up looking. Right at this imaginary plastic placemat where Shadow's food dish and his water bowl used to sit. Nothing there now. Not even the placemat.

While he was thinking that he looked up and saw Hetty gazing at that place, too, with her eyes sad. He felt bad for reminding her but at least it gave him a chance to tell her how he felt. "I'm really sorry about...you know," he said. "Shadow. Really. Jeez."

"I don't know what I'm going to do without my little guy," Hetty said, blinking back tears. She shook her head, got up, and walked over to look out of the window over the sink. "It's so ironic, since Peter found him on an esplanade in the first place, isn't it?"

"I know. You've got to wonder if it was somebody knew about that. You know? And that's why he did it exactly like that."

Hetty didn't say anything. She stood at the window, not turning around until all of a sudden Donald realized that maybe she wasn't saying anything because she couldn't. She just couldn't. He felt really terrible. He shoved at his hair. "Maybe somebody wanted to scare you into forgetting about everything. The whole deal. You know?"

As soon as the coffee started to smell good she turned away from the window and smiled at him. It wasn't much of a smile but then she held up a cup, like asking if he wanted a cup of coffee. She always did that. Donald never took her up on it but it was one of the things that she did that sort of made him feel good. One of their things. Donald shook his head., like always. She poured herself a cup and drank some coffee and dropped a couple of slices of bread into the toaster. "I don't cook much, these days but I can still make toast."

They were both quiet for a couple of minutes before Donald said, "Anybody could do that to Shadow has to be a retarded psycho."

"Beyond comprehension," Hetty said. She poured cream into a little white pitcher and put it on the table. "I'm not sure I want to know who could do such a thing. Or why."

"There's kids will do all kinds of things," Donny said. "For kicks. Mister Bach knew that, but he still kept on, you know, asking kids stuff. Trying to help them. Even the guys in the Bandidos or the Kings. He had guts."

"I know," Hetty said.

He finished the Coke and went on, "You could ask him about anything and he'd try to help you with it. He'd listen, you know?"

Hetty nodded and smiled. "Are you sure you don't want some milk?" she asked. "Or some juice?"

Donald shook his head. He took a deep breath and blurted, "Had to be some kind of a psycho. Probably supposed to make you sick." He couldn't seem to quit bringing it up.

"I rather imagine it was supposed to be sickening," Hetty said. "But you know what? It's brought me out of being sick, in a way. All along, ever since the funeral, I've been stumbling around in a fog, a kind of a sick fog. And now, I seem to be shocked awake."

She got out apple butter and honey for the toast. "You used to like both of these." When he shook his head she sat down and sipped her coffee. "I'm glad you came over."

"Me, too," Donald said. "My dad thinks it's crazy that Mrs. Albright had Mister Albright change all your locks. He can't understand how you can trust him more than us. Mister Albright's not the nicest man in the world. Mom wonders why you haven't given us a key, like always."

Hetty looked away. "I'm just not passing out keys, now that

I'm alone," she said. "Your mom and dad can understand that, surely."

"My dad's not big on any kind of understanding, ever," Donald said. "I've been looking for a part-time job. I got to get some wheels." He sighed. "Dad keeps ranting about Doris's dead-end job and yelling about wanting Mom to go up to the lake house but she's too busy, she says." He tipped his chair back. "Doris is crazy about her big deal job. She's nuts about being in on all that cop stuff. But Pop has been calling people up, trying to get her fired. You believe that? He can't handle it because it's police work. And my mom thinks it's vulgar. I guess it doesn't pay much. They want her to go to work at the *Courier.* Sell ads or whatever."

He chewed a piece of toast. "Doris talked to Mister Bach about her job. She wanted to get him to try to talk some sense into Pop. And I guess Mister Bach gave it a try, too, but lotsa luck. Pop's a mule. Me, I'm supposed to turn into some kind of overnight computer whiz. He's...my dad's full of it."

Hetty studied what was left in her coffee cup.

Donald finished a piece of toast and bit into another. "There's a lot of crap—excuse me—goes on at school," he said. "There's guys you steer clear of. Like the Dutchman. No sudden moves, no eye contact. But Mister Bach never did give a flip. He bawled out the Dutchman once for scaring some kids in the parking lot. Bawled him out in front of everybody. And you know what else? If somebody didn't give a damn about his kid, for instance, Mister Bach might have lit into him about that. Like Mister Albright? He's straightened out Mister Albright plenty of times. And my dad, too, maybe."

Hetty got up and went to the sink and stood looking down at it. "I know."

"Emily Schmulbeck is going with the Dutchman but don't say anything because her dad would croak. But he maybe saw her ride off with Clifford after the funeral, so he's probably croaking already." Donald thought about that for a couple of minutes. "I bet the Dutchman hates cats. Some of those gangsters do stuff with animals' blood, did you know that?"

Hetty came back to the table and sat down with a little thump. "Oh," she said. "Dear."

Donald wished he hadn't gone into that. He cast around for something to get past it. "Mister Cox grabs guys by their hair, sometimes," he confided. He got his voice under control and added, "Now, that's a fact. I know that because I've seen it. No kidding." Hetty looked like she believed him but it made her look even more sad.

Donald couldn't seem to get the conversation on some kind of an even keel. "I don't think he likes cats at all. In fact, I don't think Mr. Cox can stand to be around—"

"Oh, please," Hetty broke in. "Shadow always climbed all over him and Shadow wouldn't go near a cat hater. Cats know these things."

"You don't know Mr. Cox like the kids do," Donald said. "Try taking shop class sometime."

"I know you're wanting to help," Hetty said.

Donald folded his arms and looked around. He slid forward and let the chair fall back onto all four legs. "I keep trying to think who could have done it," he said. He got up and scraped his chair up under the table where it belonged and said, again, how sorry he was about what happened to Shadow.

While he was crossing to his house he heard a motorcycle start up somewhere in the subdivision.

He wished to hell he hadn't gone into all that about Emily and the Dutchman. He'd heard she was living somewhere with him now, but he had better sense than to repeat that rumor to Hetty.

Well. At least he did get to warn her about the Cocksman. Sort of. Even if she didn't want to hear it.

18

Dobie High School

Hetty kept telling herself she had to find a job, somehow take charge of her life, get going at something, but it kept raining. On August fifteenth, a Thursday, it rained hard off and on all day, with the television beeping yellow trailers warning of flash flooding. Galveston got a foot of rain, the most the island had had in more than a century. "The streets are rivers," a newscaster said jovially. "This is a good day to stay home if you can."

The *Chronicle* was depressing. A Methodist minister, a man the neighbors found loving and gentle, was charged with beating his wife to death. The wife had been "a gifted musician," the paper said. The reporter compared the murder to a bludgeoning by another minister, a man his friends called "gentle." Hetty crumpled the paper and threw it in the trash but the three main TV channels were exploring various trials and murders too, following up on "Four dead in separate shootings." Hetty could see Lieutenant Gray's sorrowing eyes, hear his voice warning her to not interfere, to let him do his job. His terrible job.

Area schools were getting ready for the fall semester, the paper said.

*

On Monday morning, Hetty got dressed and drove to Dobie High school to talk to Barbara Schwartz. She knew it would be difficult, but she had everything under control until the secretary in the outer office almost tipped over her chair jumping up to give her a hug. "Oh, Mrs. Bach," she said. "He was such a sweetie, wasn't he? Everybody feels so terrible and you're so brave and we all—-we all feel so—oh, what are we going to *do*, now?"

Hetty walked into Barbara's office with her eyes swimming. Barbara came around the desk, closed the door to her office and held Hetty to her big bosom for minutes.

Things were okay until Hetty explained why she was there, that she hoped to get some help from someone, anyone, to try to find out what had happened to Peter in that field.

"You're sleuthing?" Barbara backed away to stand with her arms crossed, leaning back against her desk. She stood looking down at Hetty while the clock on the office wall ticked and jumped from minute to minute. Hetty focused on the stacks of papers in wire baskets on the desk in front of her. Barbara had a paperweight with antlers on it that said, "The Buck stops here."

"We loved him, too, you know," Barbara said. "How can I help?"

"Oh, this is so much harder than I thought it would be," Hetty said. "I don't know. I don't know. I don't know what to do. I have to do something but I don't know what. I keep driving out there to look at that field and there's nothing there." She shook her head, determined not to cry. "I can't stop thinking about it. I keep trying to remember what Peter said, that day. Who he was going to meet. I don't think he told me. I don't know that he meant to make a big mystery of it, but he was shaving and I wasn't paying attention and I can't remember." She had to stop babbling. "I have to do something. That's all."

"I see," Barbara said.

"There must be something, some thing, that the police wouldn't think of and I feel as though it happened here? I just want a few minutes with anyone who might—"

"Who might know something?" Barbara inhaled deeply. "You do know I can't let you go roaming around here by yourself, don't you, Het?" She tried to soften that. "The police have talked to all of us. Too thoroughly. It really might be a good idea to let them handle it. You're not much of a slugger even when you're yourself."

"I'm myself." Hetty's chin started, oh God, to tremble. "If I'm going to find out anything, I'm going to have to bother people. I *have* to, Barbara. The lieutenant who's working on the case says to leave it to him but he's so overworked, he can't possibly keep trying to find out what happened. Do you realize what a violent town this is?"

Barbara looked at her.

"I know you do," Hetty said. "It begins here, doesn't it?"

Barbara sighed. "It begins in the cradle. Before then." She ran a hand through her hair. "Those three sixteen-year-olds who saw that awful thing came forward and volunteered. They've been thoroughly questioned several times." She leaned forward and pinned Hetty with her dark, piercing eyes. "We don't have any one here that I know of who knows anything. I'm not saying there aren't kids here who are capable of almost anything. Anything at all. I've got a six-foot-four inch jolly green giant in the eleventh grade who's gonna be for*ever* in the eleventh grade if he doesn't self destruct or somebody doesn't blow him away. But the cops know all about him and they're watching him and his Mexican Mafia, his Bandidos, like you wouldn't believe."

Hetty dabbed at her eyes and nodded. "I know. Clifford Van Huys. But Clifford was in San Antonio on Memorial Day."

"That he was." Barbara sat down and stood up again. "With most of his gang. Maybe all of them. Though they can be hard to keep track of." She frowned. "Clifford and his royal band. Hetty, the gang thing isn't anything to fool with. Trust me. These kids don't go around dancing and singing 'Maria.' We're trying to educate 'em but some of these kids aren't interested. They're thinking survival.

"But that's not what you need to hear. Aw, Hetty, I wish I could help. I honestly can't think of anything you or I can do that the police haven't thought of, can you?" Barbara's shoulders sagged. "Would you like a cup of coffee or a Coke or something? I'm a little dry."

"Wait," Hetty said. "I've been thinking. What if it wasn't a gangster or a thug or some enemy, out in that field? What if it was a friend? He wouldn't have meant to truly injure Peter. He might not have meant to hit him. But it happened. And Peter fell against that truck." She hugged herself. "Oh, it's so awful. I remember a time when Peter was talking about kids in a parking lot, cheering on a couple of youngsters having a fist fight. He said something about how men hit each other all the time in all our living rooms,

The Field

on the television, and the men who are struck down simply get up and straighten their ties and walk away." She cleared her throat. "Only in the real world, they don't. Do they?"

Barbara was looking at the floor.

"It might have been someone who loved him," Hetty said, swallowing. "One of us. Or a parent, worried sick or--or jealous because his son or daughter had been coming to talk to Peter. Someone frantic about grades. And he lost his temper. And this awful thing happened." She had to make Barbara understand. "This thing just happened. It happened. To him, too. To this person."

"Maybe it was a teacher," Barbara said. "Those committee meetings can get pretty bitter. And he won all those golden apples. Oh, Hetty. You can't keep surmising. What if you're right? This person has to be suffering. But let the police do their job."

Hetty nodded miserably.

It was maddening to fall apart in front of Barbara Schwartz. After she was able to stop crying, Hetty let Barbara walk her to her car.

"I see you're still driving old Clara," Barbara said, in quiet approval. "If you start running into any trouble with her, you bring her around and let our Mr. Cox and his auto technician- in-training work on a real car. Don't you know those kids would love to get their hands on a real car? They resurrected that truck that Kent brought in, though I see he finally treated himself to a Toyota. That's it, parked over next to his office, over there." She indicated metal storage building on a far corner of the lot. "These temporary buildings are awful. Thank God we're almost past all this construction."

"Awful," Hetty said, as Kent Cox opened the door of the building, waved at them and came striding across the parking lot.
He gathered Hetty to his big chest, asking, jovially, "What are you doing here?"

"Oh, Kent," Hetty said, suddenly fighting more tears. "I wish I knew." She sniffled and punished her nose with her handkerchief, fighting for composure, while Kent Cox and Barbara behaved as though they were completely accustomed to having people stand around and cry out loud in their parking lot.

"Goes with the territory," Barbara said, staring down three Hispanic youngsters. "Good afternoon, Mister Cifuentes. Mister Garcia. Mister Rodriguez."

"Vamoose," Kent said, unwinding his long arms from around Hetty. "Pronto."

Hetty finally got everything under control and got into Clara and drove out of the parking lot amid crescendos of noisy cars and motorcycles. She drove home shaking, so mad at herself she was sick to her stomach.

That was the only time Hetty went over to the high school.

She did keep going back to the field, out on Telephone Road. There was nothing to see, but she couldn't seem to stop driving out there. She didn't go to the cemetery. She went to the field and parked and sat there, or got out and walked around, just looking.

*

All through the muggy days of September and into the golden days of October, Peg grew more and more fiercely insistent about wanting Hetty to sell the house and come to live with her and the boys. Peg kept coming up with schemes for businesses they could go into, ways they could make money, share expenses. For once in her life, Peg was being completely practical. And she was right, of course. Selling the house would remove a financial burden from Hetty.

Much as she loved Peg and her sons, Hetty didn't want to live with anyone. She realized that Peg had a point: neither of their houses was paid for. By themselves, neither Hetty nor Peg had great prospects for reducing their debt. Hetty knew she ought to be worried about such things but she couldn't seem to concentrate.

The first Sunday in October she told Peg and George Gordon that she had decided to attend a grief support group that they'd been trying to get her to join, at the Presbyterian church.

She started to go to the church to the meeting, but she overshot the church and got as far as Blackhawk Drive before she turned the car around and drove up Scarsdale Boulevard to the beginning of the Southbelt hike and bike trail, a four-mile pathway that led alongside a drainage ditch to circle a catch basin surrounded by pines. She pulled into the parking lot and watched a couple of women with spaniels come off the trail, laughing and chattering.

The women looked pleasantly companionable. Hetty got out

of Clara, locked her, and started up the black-topped trail.

Insects buzzed and hummed. A froth of white bloom and tall, drying weeds edged in hectic red shone in slanted golden light. The setting sun hung low in a hazy sky, flickering through a chiaroscuro of trees off to her right.

A couple of joggers came panting by, one of them complaining about having made the circle up and around the basin at the end of the trail twice. A girl on a pink bike slowed as she approached and pumped on past. A couple with a German Shepherd sauntered up, facing Hetty.

Everybody was facing her. Nobody seemed to be setting out in her direction.

About a mile and a half along, the path wound past a clump of cottonwoods. Three elderly women and a man walking a limping poodle came walking toward her. "Getting kind of late," the man called out, as they came abreast. "You might be heading the wrong way, lady." The women nodded and chimed in. "Gets dark in a hurry, out here."

Hetty smiled. Advice, even here. She said she'd turn around in a moment.

As she came to a bend beyond a stand of live oaks she had the trail all to herself. Insects shrilled and clattered. Soughing pines edged the catch basin. Long beards of Spanish moss swayed in a freshening, cottony, evening breeze. Hetty walked faster, breathing in the scent of wild jasmine from the surrounding trees. A brown rabbit came out of a swampy area and sat perfectly still in the mowed place next to the path. He sat erect, very still. His buttony eyes gleamed as Hetty passed.

A flight of birds lifted and settled in a chinaberry tree.

She made the turn around at the basin and was on her way back when the sun dropped out of sight. .

There was no twilight. One minute she was moving through a golden haze, thinking about the stillness of the rabbit, like a small statue in the shadows, and the next she was stepping hesitantly through dense, starless darkness. She moved along more quickly, stepping cautiously, telling herself it was okay, she really had wanted to be alone and she'd soon be back at the parking lot.

Something fluttered and rattled and shrieked in the shrubbery almost at her feet. It was very dark. Very. And she wasn't alone.

Someone else seemed to be moving along on the path somewhere behind her. There was the faint snick of soles on the blacktop back there.

As the steps neared, Hetty thought it might be a good idea to let her pursuer know that there was somebody in the way. She called out an uncertain quivery, "Hi."

There was no answer. The steps came closer.

A jogger, she told herself. Somebody who'd been running and had tired; walking, now, slowing down and caught out in the dark, as uncomfortable as she was, feeling along with her feet, wishing a cloud would part and let in some moonlight, how could it have gotten so dark so suddenly?

The steps hesitated.

She moved faster.

The steps quickened.

She moved on, trying to hurry. The steps behind her matched hers, step for step, moving faster as she moved faster, slowing as she slowed.

There seemed to be several people moving along behind her. Hetty stepped up her pace until she was running.

The steps kept coming closer.

She slowed, panting, and stepped off the blacktop to carefully, stealthily tread on the grass, but it was dried and patchy and her feet made crackling noises. She moved along, stumbling now and then, feeling along the ground with her feet, hurrying—-her throat and chest hurting—

—and realized, with a cold prickle, that there was a shuffling sound that might have been a small animal moving in the dried weeds, very close behind her. The shrilling and humming and buzzing of insects had gone silent. It was so still that she could hear something in the weeds and the dark, liquid sound of something slithering into the swampy catch basin behind her. But she didn't hear any footsteps.

Then she did. In front of her and behind her, on the grass. Her pursuers had left the path, too.

19

I'm being ridiculous, Hetty told herself.

No. Someone is back there.

Maybe he's not oh maybe it's not even a he maybe it's a girl oh God let it be a girl a nice sweet girl caught out here in the dark scared to death with her heart slamming around inside her ribs the way mine is please God please.

Her foot slid on a stone. She threw out her arms, fighting for balance. A hand grabbed her arm above the elbow. Hard. She yelped.

The grip tightened, tightened again. She could feel the flesh beneath her skin soften and break under the squeezing fingers. She screamed.

There was a hot breathy sound that might have been a laugh. "Let *go*."

Hetty slumped. Let herself go limp. Threw her head back.

It connected. Her head cracked against what felt like a chin. Her assailant snorted and exhaled, an angry cat sound, hot with rage. It made her scream.

Something—the heel of a hand?—something hard slammed into her back. She sprawled, biting the inside of her cheek, her hands and knees raking through stubble and embedded stones and thorny weeds as she slid down. A rough place tore at her knee.

She screamed again. The scream turned into gasping words. "Kill me, I don't care. I'm not a person anyway I'm half of a person now—"

Her mouth filled. She swallowed and hugged herself, shaking, coughing a cough that rasped into a retching shriek. "I. Do. Not. Care," she screamed, pounding the ground, pounding her arms and chest, shrieking.

She ran out of breath.

Sat up.

Her shrieks seemed to echo. A yelping siren filled the air and resounded. The bitten place in her cheek hurt exquisitely. It tasted of salty blood. Her knees throbbed. The siren sounded very near. The sky lightened above some nearby trees. She got to her feet. A cool small breeze moved across the damp tendrils of hair on the back of her neck.

Insects shrilled.

Hetty scrambled back to the path. She could see it now, dimly, a shade darker than the surrounding grasses, mottled with moonlight. She stood bent over, her hands on her trembling knees, spitting away the coppery taste of blood, listening—

—oh, listening—

—to the sound of feet slapping their way down the path ahead of and behind her until they were lost in the williwaw of the siren, closer now, becoming an urgent nearby series of screams in an adjacent subdivision.

As she made her way back the siren's cry faded and became one of the sounds of the night, like the rattle of feathers in a nearby stand of cottonwoods and the shrilling crescendos of cicadas in the rustling weeds.

Hetty was—alone.

She limped back to the parking lot with her knees oozing warm blood.

As she came around the bend to the lighted lot she stopped and left the path to step behind an oak. There was only one other car out there in the lot, parked between her and Clara, gleaming under the greenish vapor light.

With someone on its far side.

Hetty's heart was starting to hammer again when a car door slammed on the far side of the vehicle and Kent Cox came around it, lifting his big, bony knees in the beginning of a trot. He moved clumsily, his elbows out, hurrying, until he saw her.

He stopped. His big head swung forward. "That you, Hetty?" He coughed and caught his breath. "My gosh, what in the world do you think you're doing out here all by yourself at this time of night?"

"Oh, Kent," Hetty said, whimpery with relief, "what are *you* doing here?"

"I passed you earlier, when you first got here, a while back," he said. "Why, look at you!" He caught his breath. "Are you all right? I was on my way home. Looked over and saw your car. Then I got home and found out I'm out of dog food, so I had to come back to the grocery and, gee, here's your car, still out here in the dark. So I said to myself, 'What's that girl doing out here all by her lonesome?' I was about to come looking for you. What do you think you're doing walking around out in the dark, lady?"

Hetty moved past him to lean, briefly, against the front of his car, warm and still ticking, a good, solid mass between her and the black opening in the trees behind her. "Getting bloodied," she said, breathlessly. "But unbowed." She tried for a laugh but the laugh came out sounding like a sob and there was Kent, gathering her to his chest, summoning the police on his cell phone.

Explaining to the police became embarrassing. They couldn't seem to understand why she had been walking alone, in the dark, out on the trail. It was a relief to have them get back into their busy talking-to-itself car and drive away.

Kent followed her home, of course. Her knees looked terrible, which was sort of satisfying, since they felt terrible, but they were just skinned and bruised. "Nothing a little soap and water won't fix," Hetty said, trying to dismiss Kent.

He didn't want to leave. He went to the kitchen while she laved and treated her wounds and was still there, in his torn off jeans that showed his hairy, too-thin legs, straddling a kitchen chair, when she came downstairs.

The tattered Nikes knotted with broken laces on his big feet were filthy. Those shoes really ought to be thrown away, Hetty thought, but there's nobody to tell him that.

He seemed touchingly glad to be in her kitchen. He said her bandaged knees made him think of that time she'd fallen off her bike and he'd been the one who drove her to the emergency room. "You had a broken arm and you kept saying it was nothing," he said, smiling at her. "Got mad at me for taking you to the hospital. You can be tough, for such a delicate type."

"It was a green stick fracture," Hetty said. She didn't particularly care for being called delicate and she didn't want to sit around reminiscing but she felt as though she ought to at least offer the man a cup of coffee. Then she made the mistake of asking him if he'd like a piece of toast. That led to her getting out a jar of apple butter, which seemed to make Kent's brown eyes go liquidly fervent. "Oh, you remember how I feel about apple butter."

He got out his own plate.

"You going to tell those detectives about all this?" he asked, with his mouth full. Hetty said she rather imagined that the police talked to each other pretty much but yes, she supposed she would be talking to Lieutenant Gray. Kent chewed and swallowed. "Don't you wish he'd speak up?" he said. "He's got to be a lot brighter than I think he is. Those boys have got to be pretty busy. Two hundred and sixty-seven homicides in Houston last year and we've got a running start so far this year, according to the *Chronicle*. Last time I talked to them they were asking about Jerry Albright, for cryin' in the bucket."

"Jerome?" Hetty swallowed a nervous yawn. "Oh, dear. That's all Peg needs. I don't know why Jerome would hurt Peter."

Kent shrugged. "Maybe Peter told him to stay away from some high school girl."

"Oh, poor Peg," Hetty said. "I don't want to think about it."

Kent chewed and swallowed. "Yeah. He's a couple of sandwiches short of a picnic." He got up and put more bread in the toaster. "You still haven't explained what you were doing out on the trail in the dark."

"It wasn't dark when I started out," Hetty said. "It got dark unbelievably fast. Now I know what people mean when they talk about how dark it can be in a cave." She rubbed her arm.

Kent glanced down at his big-knuckled hands. He folded them and looked up at her from under his heavy eyebrows. "Well. Hell of a thing."

"You haven't told me about the fire at your place," she said.

Kent grinned. "You heard about that? Wasn't much to it. I had a little altar rigged up with a cloth and some candles and Milo pulled on the thing and tipped the candles over. And some wag called the fire department. I had it out before they showed up. Pretty weird, huh? I told Milo, 'Hey, dog. Aren't you supposed to be man's best friend?'"

His head sagged forward and he looked up at Hetty, sorrowing. "Way I see it, Pete was my best friend. I kept wanting to get him up to the lake and now he never will make it. It's so pretty up there, Hetty. Dave and Louise never use the place. They're just keeping it as some kind of an investment and you ought to see the hardwoods and the water. There's a pier. I don't suppose you'd ever let me take you up there? You could bring your watercolors. Set up your easel and— "

He looked as if he realized he'd gone too far and started to stammer. "After you get past this, I mean. We wouldn't have to stay over. What I do is get up before dawn and take off early and beat the traffic. Hardly any traffic, even on holidays, if you get going early enough."

His face unclouded and went sweetly eager. "Sa-ay," he said, snapping his fingers, "you know what? What we need to do is get up before it gets so hot out and start walking on the hike and bike trail, once in a while. Milo loves that. And the thing is, it looks to me like you could sure use some company." He smiled. "No point in your going out all by your lonesome, even in the daylight. I'd like to start doing that. Milo loves it out there. He doesn't get enough exercise."

Hetty got up and put the milk back in the refrigerator. "That's something to think about," she said.

"This has got to be the worst time for you, Hetty," he said. "You don't want to go around playing detective." A drop of milk in his beard caught the light every time his chin moved. He sounded tremulous. "Now, Dave says you keep running around stirring things up and you've got to be about half crazy with grief. You're apt to stumble into some damned thing and...." He lifted his hands in helpless consternation. "You don't want to do that. Don't know what you might be dealing with. You could get yourself hurt."

"Is that what David says? I'm already hurt." Hetty put their cups in the sink. She looked out of the window over the sink and glanced up at the clock. "You don't want that dog of yours to languish and starve," she said.

Kent stumbled to his feet and sat back down. "I probably shouldn't tell you this, honey," he said, "but, as a matter of fact, Dave Gofor and I have had a long talk with his boy, Donald, and those other two friends of his."

Hetty turned to stare at him.

"That's right," Kent said, nodding. "Dave and I got those kids off in a corner and guess what? Those boys, hell, honey, those boys don't know diddly. They got that license plate number all bollixed up. A couple of them told the cops that truck was a Mazda and Donny thought, for a spell there, that it might be that Ford they turned over to the school for my kids to work on. That truck wasn't much and it got stolen," Kent said. "Months ago. Some kids probably took it for a joy ride and couldn't keep it running long enough to get it back. I figured it wasn't worth getting the kids in Dutch."

"So I've been told." Hetty's knee hurt. Her arm hurt. Her mouth hurt. Being polite was beginning to take more effort than it was worth.

"David's worried about his boy and I don't blame him. Scared of his own shadow. Those detectives are checking up on Dave and what I figure is, it's got to be because of that Nervous Nelly kid of his. I wish he'd take that boy fishing," he said. "Well, I guess you want to turn in."

By the time Kent went down the walk to his car, the overcast had become dense enought to shroud the street lights. He stood out in the driveway in the fog for so long that Hetty drew the blinds and turned away, yawning, thinking that he'd be getting damp out there if he didn't just get in his car and go away.

The next morning all her bruised places felt wretched. She needed aspirin. She went out and unlocked Clara and started to get in and stopped. The driver's seat had a crumpled dampish sheet of blue lined notebook paper pressed into its creases. Someone had left a message printed in black Marks-A-Lot: "Leave it alone."

Oh, this must have been here last night, she thought. I must have driven all the way from the hike and bike trail with my poor aching rump settling into this portentous message. And I didn't feel a thing.

20

Lieutenant Gray thought she was far too casual about being attacked on the trail and the warning note left in Clara, but Hetty told him she didn't think there was any real virtue in dwelling on such things.

"What am I to do? Hide? Run away? Someone wants me to quit poking around," she told him. "And isn't that what you keep saying you want, too? You keep suggesting I leave the driving to you. I think I'll leave the worrying to you, as well."

On Halloween night, however, she wished Lieutenant Gray was around or that she had taken Peg up on her offer to come over to her house when the back door started shaking. Hetty backed away and picked up the phone as she watched the antique brass knob twist and turn. After a couple of minutes, the whole door rattled. "I'm calling the police," she yelled, trying to sound threatening.

"That you, Hetty?" Kent Cox asked. "Something's the matter with my darned key."

"I've changed the locks," Hetty said. She opened the door. Kent had both arms around a damp and sagging grocery sack with a stalk of celery sticking out of the top and a silly conical black hat on. Kent always had something of a chubby elfin look anyway, Hetty thought, and his Halloween hat completed the look. Tufts of his dark hair were plastered to his sweaty brown and sticking out around the bottom of the silly hat. "You look like a gnome," she said. "Did you have to pick Halloween to try to use your old key? Why didn't you knock?"

"Been knocking," Kent said. "Where've you been? Trick or treat! Thought I'd surprise you with a little supper. How come you didn't answer your door? And there aren't any cars in your garage.

Where's Clara?"

The front door bell chimed. "The Ford's in the shop," Hetty said, "and I parked out in front. I was in a hurry. There are all these children." She went to answer the front door.

As soon as she came back, the front doorbell chimed again.

"You'd better get that," Kent said. "I'll just take some of this stuff out of the bag, here. I was over at Randall's and I guess I thought you might enjoy some supper and—you changed the locks? Now why'd you go and do that? Somebody been bothering you?"

He brushed past her so he could thump the grocery sack onto the kitchen table. It fell over. A little wooden container of brie rolled out and he picked it up and started tossing it from hand to hand. "Want me to do the honors?"

Hetty answered the front door and distributed candy.

When she came back Kent was setting out slices of ham and cheese and two kinds of crackers. "Thought we might put together a little supper, since you don't seem to ever want to go out with anybody these days." He looked at her and his smile faded. "Ham? And, you know, cheese? What could that hurt?"

He looked so moist-eyed and desperately friendly that it was a relief when the front door bell chimed again so she could go attend to it. When she returned Kent said, "Why don't we have a cup of coffee to go with this? Brought you some almond flavored coffee. I seem to remember you and Pete always liked this almond flavored coffee."

"I'm going to spend this entire evening doling out goodies," Hetty said. "Sit down. Oh, Kent. I've been by myself so much I scarcely know how to be hospitable. I usually drink tea but the coffee maker's right where it's always been. Why don't you help yourself."

He gave a crestfallen shrug. "Oh, tea, that's right. You're a tea sip. Earl Grey with cream and sugar. I knew that." His face brightened. "I did bring milk." He held up a cardboard milk container. Milk dripped down his sleeve. "Guess I bounced this around, some. I think it's sprung a leak."

Hetty got out a pitcher. Kent dumped the milk into it. As she put the pitcher in the refrigerator, the doorbell chimed and she turned abruptly to find Kent in her way. They both moved to the right and

The Field

left before she could get past him.

He followed her through the house to the front hall. "Maybe what you need is a hug," he said.

Hetty let herself be hugged in the front hall as the door bell chimed insistently. Kent didn't seem to want to let go of her. All sorts of people had been hugging her for the past several months but this felt so very awkward that she backed away, slightly off balance, groped behind her and found a chair back but the chair tilted, sending her even more foolishly off balance. She turned around, righted the chair and opened the door, more than a little annoyed.

When she got back to the kitchen Kent was sitting quietly at her table, musing over a cup of coffee. He glanced up at her and said, "Been missing you, Hetty. You shouldn't close out your friends at a time like this."

When she didn't answer he got up and busied himself unloading the rest of the groceries on the counter next to the sink. The bag split, spilling a box of mushrooms onto the table. "I've learned how to make cream of mushroom soup with mushrooms and cream and Campbell's Cream of Mushroom soup," he said. "You just fry the mushrooms in butter and add them to—well, I guess you get the idea. You can do that with celery soup, too. You just add fresh celery. And potato soup, same, same. Nothing to it. I'm getting to be quite a chef."

"Well, don't tell Peg," Hetty said. "She'll want to go into business with you. Peg is madly looking for any sort of enterprise to go into." It made her sigh. "And she keeps wanting me to join her."

Kent smiled through a frown. "Oh, honey. You shouldn't have to be thinking about things like that at a time like this."

"I'm going to have to think about such things," Hetty said and immediately wished she hadn't. Kent looked as though he might be readying an embarrassingly intimate response. "You guys took care of me," he started in. "Might be my turn to—" but the doorbell chimed. Saved by the bell, she thought.

"This looks like a lot of food," Hetty said, when she came back again.

Kent nodded. "Aren't you hungry?"

She wasn't, very. She ate some of Kent's tinned cream of mushroom soup with fresh mushrooms in it and some of the crackers with the pate but it was hard to chew and swallow with Kent gazing so soulfully.

After a time his brow furrowed. "This may not be the best idea I've ever had," he said. "But you don't seem so uncomfortable having that Gofor kid over here or that lieutenant."

Hetty gave him a long look and he went slightly pink.

"Well, hell, Hetty. Nothing wrong with your friends kind of keeping an eye on this place, is there?" He seemed to have some difficulty swallowing a bit of cracker. "You want to be careful of all teenagers right about now," he said, coughing.

"Donald Gofor tells me you were in town on Memorial Day," Hetty said. When Kent's brow creased she went on. "You weren't up at the lake, were you?"

"Did I say I was up at the lake?"

She nodded. "I think you did. But Donald said he saw you selling snow-cones?"

He winced. "I guess I didn't want anybody to know about that little situation. I bought that snow-cone truck but it's not all that profitable." He shrugged, embarrassed. "Yeah, I ran that cart on the holiday. Big deal. That little shit couldn't wait to run around telling people, huh?"

"I don't know as he's telling too many people," Hetty said. "It sort of came up. Donald is—"

"—a little shit."

He got up to pace around. "Turned out to be not such a great idea. The snow-cone thing, I mean. I sold that contraption today. That's what this celebration is about. Cashed the check and went to Randall's and then I thought about you, about how everybody says you've quit eating and, well, you don't have that much padding to spare, Hetty honey."

Hetty stiffened and lifted her chin. "Would you care for more coffee?" she asked. "Or—oh, dear. Look at the time. It is getting a bit late, isn't it?"

Kent took the hint but he was forever getting to the door and once he got there he lingered, unburdening himself further. "I didn't lie about being out of town to the cops. I guess I just didn't see any reason to make a point of where I was to...to my friends. Aw, Hetty.

The Field

You don't want to keep poking around at, you know, what happened to Pete. That might just have been some kid, and, well, you've got to remember that even rotten kids have families."

He sighed. "You ought to see the kids I see. Kids can do lousy things but then some of them grow up and turn out to be all right. Whoever did that to Peter, well, he's probably already punishing himself worse than anybody else could punish him, don't you think?"

Hetty bit her tongue.

He got as far as the walk before he turned around and came back. "You want me to run along, I'll run along. But Hetty, I have to know: you don't think for a minute that I ever would have hurt Pete, do you? I wouldn't, you know. We had our differences. I've got kind of a short fuse once in a while but it's all fuss and noise. I wouldn't ever set out to seriously hurt our boy, you do know that, don't you?"

Hetty said she knew that. "But the man who hit him might not have meant to have things go so terribly wrong." She touched his outstretched hand. "I've thought of that. Somehow it's good to know that you feel that way, too. One of your dearest qualities is your gentleness, Kent."

Kent frowned. "You could be right about how someone might not have meant to...to do that to Pete," he said, finally. "It's been my experience that passive people can be amazingly dangerous. They're the ones you have to look out for. They never really mean to do anything. They let things happen. Or things sort of happen through them, do you know what I mean?" Just thinking about it made his mouth tighten. "They just sort of attract trouble." His head was swaying. "Kind of like water seeking its own level."

Once he'd finally walked down the walk, gotten into his noisy car and driven away, Hetty locked the front and back doors, glad to be finished with Halloween.

*

The next day, a Friday, November first, she drove over to Becker's Books to see if she could find an out-of-print cookbook that Peg said she would like to have, for Thanksgiving.

She was comfortably browsing among the other browsers, lost in Annie Dillard's marvelous *Pilgrim at Tinker Creek* when the pleasant hum of conversation all through Becker's nooks and crannies stopped. The store went so silent that she looked up, startled. There was an electric feel to the air, as if a switch had been pulled somewhere in the front of the store. Hetty dropped the Annie Dillard novel on top of the three books stacked at her feet and straightened to rub the small of her back, wondering what was happening. The power hadn't gone off. The hum of an air conditioning unit in the wall near her seemed loud. It hadn't begun to rain. Dust motes danced in the rays of sunlight streaming through a small window at her right.

She stepped into a hall, trudged up a ramp and turned right into narrow back corridor. That corridor dead ended in cookbooks and travel. She looked at a couple of cookbooks and turned to retrace her steps and a glowering stranger, a tall teenager with complexion troubles, stepped into the hall and leaned against the door jamb, blocking her way. He didn't say anything. He just stood there, not looking at her, looking indolent and annoyed or possibly those eyelids always drooped at half mast over those almond shaped eyes. He must be very warm in that leather vest and the checkered headband, Hetty thought. His chest, naked beneath the open vest, shone with perspiration.

When she breathed a startled, "Hi," he edged a bit closer and leaned against the wall.

"Well, hi," Hetty said again, and, after a moment, "Excuse me?"

The almond eyes flickered in her direction and slid away. He seemed not to have heard.

"Are you looking for something in particular?" Hetty tried to sound genial. "It's so easy to get lost in here, isn't it?"

"Lost?"

She seemed to be off on the wrong foot. "Well, I mean, this place is a series of labyrinths, isn't it?"

His brows drew together in a scowl.

She waited for him to say something more. He didn't.

After a minute or two, she said, "Well, I guess I've found everything I want." She stepped forward. He didn't budge. "Excuse me?" Evidently he didn't realize what she meant. Hetty managed what she hoped would look like a smile. "Habla usted Espanol?" That may have been a mistake.

The Field

His lip curled.

She inhaled and exhaled. This lad had to be a teenager. She knew that sullen look. She and Pete had dealt with that, on all kinds of levels, for years. Pete used to call it Donny's "leave me alone" look. Donny would come stamping across the street, bored and resentful and mad at the world to stand in the kitchen doorway, and Pete would say, "Uh oh," and sometimes it would be "Uh oh" for half an hour or more. Other boys had come around with that look, too; football players worried about a passing grade; one awful day there'd been a boy that the manager of Walgreen's had caught with two cameras in his pocket. Peter had worked with that lad for weeks, off and on.

This pimply young man was no child, however. He had a dragon wrestling with a largish bird tattooed on his chest and ripples of distinct musculature shone, up and down his bulging biceps. Hetty thought it might be best to ignore him.

He didn't like being ignored. "Joo think I don' spik Engles?" he said. He spat on the floor. Hetty looked down at the wet place on Becker's lovely wooden floor. When she looked up, he bent to select a book from the shelf, and, his eyes holding hers, lifted a page by one corner and ripped it straight across. He was beginning to tear another page when Hetty couldn't help herself. "Oh, please."

"Joo don' like that?"

There was really no point in confronting him. She backed away.

He took another, heavier book from the shelf and was shoving it open when a voice from around the corner in the hall said, just above a whisper, "Cesar."

The young man's face went blank. He put the book back, shrugged and sidled away.

Clifford Van Huys stepped into the hall and stood gazing at Hetty with his head back, his pale eyes half closed, saying, quietly, "Mrs. Bach."

"Clifford," Hetty breathed. "Hi. How are you?"

"Good," Clifford said. "You?"

She drew in a shaky breath. "I'm fine. Glad to see you," she said. "Was that a friend of yours? "

"No."

"He's a vandal," Hetty said.

"Yes." Clifford's eyes had a cold glint. "I'll take care of it."

"Good." Hetty looked around. "I've never run into you here. I'm here so often that I know the stock pretty well. Are you looking for anything in particular?"

He smiled. For Clifford, that might be a smile, she thought, chilled.

"Friend's laid up," he said. The wintery smile faded altogether. Hetty did so wish Clifford could be more expansive. He'd always been so terse. She'd tried to help him with that but now it seemed to have gotten much worse. And he'd grown so...so towering.

There was a long pause and then he said, "Poems."

"Oh, your laid-up friend likes poetry," Hetty said. "The poetry section is over here, at our left, in front." She led the way. "Good of you to help your friend."

"Miss Lydia." He looked around at the books. "Miss Hampton. Used to teach this." He tilted a volume of Keats toward her and tucked it back in the crook of his arm.

Lydia, Hetty thought, casting about. Lydia. "Lydia Hampton?" she said, surprised. "How is she?" Lydia'd taught at Dobie for thirty years, a no-nonsense, fierce little person with a face like a bull dog. That Lydia. Gracious. Retired sixteen years ago, in the early stages of Parkinson's. "She must be very ill by now," Hetty murmured.

Clifford nodded. "Got a nurse."

Hetty could imagine what that must be like, fiercely independent little Lydia, hibernating in that greenish old house on the bayou in Friendswood, under a nurse's care. But Lydia did love to read. "How good that she has you," she said. "Here we are. These are alphabetical, by poet, and here are the anthologies. Want some help?"

Clifford smiled at her. She rather wished he wouldn't do that. She pressed her lips in a line but couldn't quite manage a credible smile. It took an effort of will to still the trembling in her hands. She found two of Billy Collins's collections and Seamus Heaney's new *Beowulf* and was considering a Yeats when Clifford said, "You need to look out for Mister Kent."

The remark surprised her. "Why do you say that?"

He shrugged. "He's a liar."

Hetty studied the books on the shelf in front of her. "He may be somewhat careless with the truth but Kent is my friend, Clifford." He nodded. "Mrs. Bach," he said. "You know what I'm saying? Look out for the Cocksman. And look out for Emily's old man."

"You're talking about my friends," Hetty said, stiffly. "Johnny Schmulbeck is a very old friend and a gentle gentleman."

"He drove over your cat," Clifford said. He looked startled as she swayed and quickly put out a hand beneath her arm to steady her. "Sorry."

"Are...are you sure?" Her mouth was dry. She didn't want to believe him.

Clifford nodded. "Saw it," he said.

"Do you think he—did he know?"

"Saw it." Clifford had his head down, little points of light in his eyes. "Hey. You gonna be okay?"

"I don't understand," Hetty said. "Why? Why would he—?"

"Runnin' scared," Clifford said. His mouth twisted in contempt.

Hetty turned away, suddenly sick with rage. She turned back and pushed at his chest, and it was like shoving at a wall.

He looked down at her, his eyes knowing, both his hands up, his hands held toward her with the palms turned up. "Sorry," he said again.

"Are you?" she said, breathing hard. "Are you ever sorry, any of you? I. Am. So. Mad. I'm so sick of all this. Why are you telling me such things?" She didn't want his help. She wanted him to go away, to be gone, before he said any more. She didn't want him to keep trying to reach for her, to keep trying to hold her up. She shoved at him and when he didn't move, put her fists against herself, against her mouth and said, through her clenched fists, "Don't you dare say that about Johnny. Don't you tell me that. I'll never believe that."

But she did. She knew he was telling the truth.

He gazed at her, sorrowing. Letting her rave.

"How could you have seen? Where were you? Why didn't you tell the police? Were you lurking around out there, outside my house, in my driveway, sneaking around? I know you've been doing that. Don't come near my house," she said, fighting tears.

"Was that one of your gangsters that threw things all over Peter's desk? Why? Don't you dare touch Peter's things, any of you, do you hear me? I've seen you out in front of the house, sitting on that motorcycle. And Lieutenant Gray has seen you. Don't you come near my house." She shoved at him, crying, hating him, hating the way she sounded. "Was that some of your henchmen, your Nomad gangsters, out on the hike and bike trail? Was it?"

He backed away. "Should never have happened," he said. "Thought they were with it, doing good, but they blew it." He shook his head. "Shouldn't have happened."

"I laughed at them," Hetty said.

"Won't happen again," he said. His eyes flared.

"Maybe it was your Cesar that killed my little Shadow," Hetty said.

"Emily's dad," Clifford said.

She leaned against a shelf, hating him, hating the way she sounded, yelping and blubbering, her nose running. She was making a spectacle of herself in Becker's book store.

"We're on it," he said. He picked up the books at his feet and shouldered his way down the hall.

She said after him, crying harder, "Johnny's my friend. Now I don't know what to do."

21

Tuesday noon Donald's starting out the door of the Dobie cafeteria, shifting around a ton of books and notebooks and papers in his backpack, late to a conference with Mr. Dickey to talk about a make-up in algebra. He's running, head down. And he runs into the Dutchman. He butts the Dutchman's chest with his damn head.

Man.

Donald steps on his feet, backing off.

After a couple of seconds he works up a shit-eating smile. He makes like going on past but the Dutchman moves around in front of him. In the doorway. Between Donald and the corridor.

A couple of kids start to edge past them to get to the corridor and change their minds.

"Get the cat," the Dutchman says.

"The cat?"

The Dutchman looks at him. Hard eyed.

"Hetty's cat? Shadow? B-b-but he's dead and buried," Donald says. "I think those kids want to get past us."

The Dutchman doesn't take his eyes off Donald.

The kids edge away.

"Hetty Bach's cat?" Donald can't believe it. "You want what's left of Hetty Bach's cat?"

The Dutchman runs his tongue over his teeth and rolls his shoulders, some. "Got it?"

Donald has to clear his throat to get his voice back. "How am I gonna do that?" He swallows and changes that, fast. "Like, how am I gonna get it to you is what I mean. Like, I mean, wh-where? And all."

"Almeda Mall."

"Yeah, sure," Donald says. "Almeda Mall. Uh, like, where?"

"In front of Bracewell." The Dutchman lifts his forearm. It's got all kinds of tattoos and those ropey veins and muscles. It takes Donald a second to realize he's supposed to be looking at the guy's watch. "Nine tonight," the Dutchman says.

"Nine o'clock is good." Donald tries not to stammer or start jabbering. "Good. Yeah. You got it." Kids are crowding around back at a table, not staring or anything. The Dutchman looks like he's running out of patience. The buzzer goes off in the corridor. Nobody moves.

"You got it," Donald says. "Right. Okay. You got it."

The Dutchman's eyes glint. "Enough." He flexes his shoulders and strolls away. The kids are trying not to stare.

That night Donald sneaks into the Bach's back yard with a spade and an empty computer paper box. He digs up Shadow. Shovels him in. The box says "Bonus Pak." Right.

Nine o'clock the Dutchman swerves into the lot in front of Bracewell in a Beemer. Donald hands him the box. He smiles. Donald wishes he wouldn't do that.

Donald starts to say something but the Dutchman holds up a finger like a kind of a salute. He half closes one eye and grunts, "Enough."

Like Donald might be getting ready to talk too much. "Enough," Donald says. "Right. You got it. Right." The Dutchman's mouth kind of pulls in at the corners and he looks at Donald with those eyes for a minute and shakes his head before he takes off.

Donald is left leaning against the Kumquat tree out in front and the lights going off inside Bracewell Library, thinking oh, man, enough, right, enough. I hope what's in that box is enough because the way I see it, it's got to be a whole hell of a lot too much.

22

Early Wednesday morning Hetty's door bell chimed four times before she could hurry downstairs and unlock the front door. She opened it a very little way and Johnny Schmulbeck slammed the door open and shoved on in. He limped past her and charged down the hall all the way through the house to the kitchen, scuffed into the rag rug in front of her rocker and kicked it against the wall. "Came over to thank you, kid," he said, his lips tight against his teeth. "Thanks a whole hell of a lot."

"F-for what?" Hetty asked him.

He snorted. "'For what?'" he said, mimicking her in a stammering falsetto. "I think you have a pretty good idea for what."

Hetty looked away from his saggy red-rimmed eyes.

"You figure it's my birthday?" he demanded. "What are you trying to pull, kid?"

Hetty backed up and sank into her rocking chair. "I know it's not your birthday. I know when you were born." Then, annoyed at the timid, foolishly querulous sound of her voice, she added, sounding sillier, "Saturday was my darned birthday and nobody remembered and I don't care. What's the matter with you?" She almost said something about how pathetic it was to smell whiskey on a man at seven o'clock in the morning but she thought better of it, since Johnny's big homely face was looming over her in furrowed confusion.

"You didn't send it," he said. He squinted at her, backed away and fell into a chair. "You have any idea what I'm talking about?"

She shook her head.

"Aw."

"Why don't I make some coffee?"

"Wait," he said. His head was in his hands. "How friendly are you with those bikers keep hanging around here? I know Pete thought some of those animals were regular Robin Hoods, salt of the earth and all that, God, he could be the most gullible son-of- a-bitch in the world sometimes, but you got to be brighter than that, I hope."

"I can't imagine what you're talking about," Hetty said. "Look. We could both use a cup of —"

"Wait," Johnny hit his brow with the heel of his hand. When she started to get up, he grabbed her wrist and yanked his chair closer. A lock of hair fell over his forehead. His eyes were intent.

After a minute or two he backed off. "Aw, no," he said, and got up to lead her over to the table and pull out a chair. When he sat down opposite her he stretched his forearms out on the table, his hands palm up, inviting her to put her hands in his. "I'm sorry," he mumbled. "I just thought..." and his voice trailed off. A small mist of wet glistened in his eyebrows and in his hair.

He looks like a sick animal, shaking his big furry head, she thought.

"You didn't send me anything?" he asked, confused.

"I did not." Hetty flashed on Clifford's warning, but this was Johnny, after all, gentle Johnny, with tears welling up in his blood-shot eyes.

"Your hands are cold," he said, gruffly. He chafed her hands gently with his big warm paws.

"Should I have sent you something?" Hetty asked.

"Had this package left on the porch," he said and hesitated. "Should have known you didn't have anything to do with it. Aw, hell, I don't know what I'm doing here."

He let go of her hands and rubbed his chin and the side of his face. "I got this package and then the cops came by. That lieutenant what's his name? Gray. Pulled up, in front. Maybe just to ask some more questions. Whatever. I didn't stick around to find out. I went out the back while Hallie was letting them in the front. Maybe they didn't have anything to do with the package, but I don't know. That Gray guy creeps me out."

He felt his chin with his knuckles. "I didn't even shave."

"A package?" Hetty asked.

Johnny sighed. "Your cat. What's left of it. Wrapped up in a shirt just like the one that—wrapped up in one of Pete's shirts. Has to be your cat. I don't know what the hell's going on. I guess one of those bikers came by and left this damn box on my porch, had this shirt, like one of Pete's Hawaiian shirts."

He got up and came around the table to hug her. "Hey, I'm sorry. Please don't look like that. Can you not look like that?"

Hetty shoved him away. She got up and paced around and sat down and got up and sat down again and went walking all around the house, walking fast, bumping into the edges of the things, trying to get away from Johnny, from what he had said.

"Oh, get away," she wept, walking, but he wouldn't leave her alone. He followed her clucking and fussing. They ended up in the front hall, sitting on the bottom step of the stairs, both of them tearful.

After Hetty had everything under control, she said, on a breath that broke in the middle, "Who would do such a thing?" She blew her nose. "Every time I think I've reached some kind of a limit someone comes around with one more thing."

"I know," Johnny said miserably. He kept rubbing his knuckles on his chin. He put his long arm around her and patted her on the shoulder. "Should've known better than to come over here. I should have known you wouldn't have a clue. I'm sorry."

"I've got to talk to Lieutenant Gray." She got up and went to the kitchen telephone with Johnny close behind.

"Aw, you don't want to do that," he said, covering her hand on the phone and lifting it off. "Let's not make a big fuss. "A spate of rain rattled against the pane of the window behind him and he turned around to look at it. When he turned back to face her he said, "My damn hip aches when it rains. You got anything to drink?"

"Johnny," Hetty said. "I think I'm beginning to understand what happened." She knew she ought to stop but she couldn't. "It was you, wasn't it?"

His face darkened.

She didn't care. She had to know.

Something slid behind his eyes. He lifted a hand and flipped it dismissively. "What a hell of a thing to say," he said. "Why would you come up with a thing like that?"

"Did you?" She had to know.

"Did I run over your cat?" His mouth pulled down.

"Shadow," Hetty whispered. "His name was Shadow."

"Of course not," Johnny said. "I could never do a thing like that and that's the truth, pure and simple—"

"Oh, my dear," Hetty said, "Dear, deranged Johnny. The truth is seldom simple and scarcely ever pure. It's almost always all muddled up and messy, isn't it?"

There was so much misery in the room she could scarcely breathe.

"You know me better than that," he said, slowly. "What's the matter with you?" He pulled his chin in and blinked accusingly. "Hell of a thing," he grumbled.

"Someone saw you," Hetty said.

He looked indignant. "And you'll believe whoever that was, instead of me, that it?" When he moved around, favoring his bad hip, knuckling his chin, Hetty could hear Donald's croaky voice, saying, "Maybe he got hurt or somethin' because the guy limped. *I* saw that much. And he had this ring." But Donald thought it was Clifford's ring, with its skull and crossbones. The ring on Johnny's left hand was his anniversary ring. The ring Hallie gave him on their fifth anniversary, that he always wore, that kept catching the light of the fixture hanging over the table now as he lifted his trembling hand to his chin, turning to stare at her because Hetty knew.

She knew.

"How could you?" she whispered.

He leaned against the wall with his rounded back to her.

"You didn't mean to do it," she heard her voice say. It sounded distantly dispassionate. "How did it happen? I have to understand."

When he turned back to her perspiration shone in the furrows of his dark face. "You're not going believe this," Johnny said. "I never meant to hurt your damned cat. The back door wasn't all the way shut so I came on in. As soon as I realized you weren't home I started to leave but then, hell, I thought I might go through the desk again, to see if there was anything, any word from Emily. She's gone off again. I didn't want to go into this. I can't talk about it, but Emily's not speaking to me. She's gone. I thought maybe she might be writing to you. She confided in Pete all the time. I don't want to talk about it."

He wiped at his chin, explaining, explaining: "Then I got some idea that I might do something, leave a note or something, to get you to quit poking around. God, you keep poking around and poking around, getting chummy with those renegade bikers and stirring up all kinds of hell. Those Bandidos. You don't know what you're doing, messing with those people. We're all of us afraid you'll get hurt, Hetty."

"So I was over at Pete's desk, looking for one of those Marks-a-lots and some paper, trying to figure out what to do and, yeah, I guess I was a couple of sheets to the wind, and then I heard the water running and you were, God, in the house and the cat started yowling and rubbing hair all over my pants and I thought, I don't know. I didn't think. And there was the carrier, sitting there, in the middle of the kitchen floor. So I shoved him in the carrier. To get him out of the way for a couple of minutes. I just wanted to shut him up and make him quit going nuts around my ankles." He was wringing his hands.

"I ran out and dropped the carrier on the drive. Then I found out I didn't have my keys. I ran back in, and while I was looking for my keys I looked out and there was this detective parked out in front. I thought he might be headed for the front door. I lost it. I went out and got in my car in a hurry and backed out." He swallowed and twisted his hands, imploring her. "Never meant to run over that thing. Shit. I was gonna stick around, try to explain, but then, like I said, there's that detective, Gray, out in front and, I swear to you, I thought I heard one of your Bandidos up the street somewhere near. I hightailed it out of there."

He paced, frowning, groping for more words.

Hetty knew that she had to go ahead and say it. Get it out in the open. "How could you?" she whispered.

"I just told you," he said. "It was an accident."

"I'm not talking about Shadow," Hetty said.

Johnny brought a shaking hand up to his mouth. "Aw, come on, now," he said, his eyes squeezing almost shut.

Hetty leaned toward him, holding on to her elbows, huddled, trying not to shake. "I think I've known for a long time," she said. "Kent loaned you his truck, didn't he? You just happened to be driving Kent's truck, that day. So he must know. Does David know?

David knows about the truck. So he must have his suspicions. But they don't want to get you in trouble, do they?"

Rain rattled the window behind him as Johnny started to weep. She got up and got the box of tissues out of the downstairs bathroom. The drumming sound of the rain increased as she let herself go on, raising her voice so Johnny could hear her. "Poor David. Poor Kent. They've been carrying this around, too, all this time. Sick with grief over losing Peter and worrying about you. Where is the truck? On the bottom of Lake Livingston?"

"Oh, what the hell is all this?" Johnny said. He moved toward her, wanting to take her hands again, trying to gather her to him. "Are you crazy?" he said. "Come on. You're sounding absolutely nuts, here. This is me, Johnny, kiddo."

She pulled away, whispering, "Why?"

He turned and walked to the kitchen door. "I'm out of here." He reached for the handle but stopped. "Hetty," he said. "Come on, kid. Don't do this to yourself. You think this over, you're gonna see how crazy you are."

"Was it because of Emily?" Hetty went on, sorting it out, talking to herself as much as to him. "It must have been. You and Hallie tried so hard to keep her from the world but she's leaving you now, isn't she? Did you somehow blame Peter for that?" She remembered something. "Peter said she 'trod so sweetly it were as on a cloud.'"

"Yeah," Johnny said. He came back and sat across from her. "Pete came up with that kind of crap, but he was the one told her to take charge of her life, go where she wants, get out from under my thumb—he said that. My thumb. My fine firm thumb, he calls it. Tells her it's okay to get in with that gang of lousy bikers and he's the one who——What are we doing, Hetty? We don't want to go into all this."

He wiped his eyes. "He's gone. Pete's gone. And now she is, too. Emily. She might as well be dead. That's how gone she is."

He got up and paced in a circle. When he came back and dropped into the chair, his voice sounded more normal. "Give me a minute and I'll go over the whole damned thing. Things aren't exactly the way you think." He closed his eyes and opened them and gazed at her blearily. "You got anything to drink?"

Hetty went to the refrigerator and lifted out a carton of tomato juice but Johnny flipped his hand. "I mean a *drink* drink." He came over and towered over her, getting down a squat glass from the top shelf of the cupboard. "It's in the dining room, right? Shall I get it?"

Hetty went into the dining room and got Peter's holiday Dewar's out of the buffet. The bottle had a film of dust on it. She swiped at it with her skirt and brought it into the kitchen.

Johnny sloshed some into a glass. "Don't suppose you'll join me?"

"I could do with a drop," Hetty said.

He smiled and made a little face at her, feigning amiable surprise. "Well, well, what have we here? A drinking companion?"

He tossed most of drink down and poured another.

Hetty sipped at her drink and held it to the light. How strange he looks, she thought. Sad and old. A sad old man.

"In the first place I couldn't ever hurt Peter," he said. "I couldn't hurt anybody but especially not Pete. How long have you known me? Have I ever hurt anybody you know of? Ever? You know who's the one with a mean temper. And his old man slapping him around, making him take up boxing. Jesus."

Hetty nodded. She knew about Kent's father and the boxing lessons. She didn't want to talk about Kent. She took a sip and inhaled, holding the whiskey in her mouth, determined not to sputter. When it went burning down her throat she couldn't restrain a cough. Once she'd begun choking and coughing, she couldn't stop. Johnny got up and pounded gently between her shoulder blades. He moved around, restlessly, until she had things under control.

"Kent would never hurt Peter," Hetty said.

"But I would?" Rain gusted against the window. Johnny smiled sadly. "Well, you're wrong," he said. "Kent would never set out to hurt Peter. He'd never mean to hurt Pete. Or you, or me, or any of us. Just like you or I would never want to get Kent in trouble, would we? What would it take to make you want to hurt a guy like Kent, loves you as much as he does, all these years?"

Johnny was hoarse with exhaustion. "I'm not the one the guys are protecting. You got it straight up wrong, honey. You ready to listen?"

23

Johnny Schmulbeck

"Kent wanted Peter to meet him out on Telephone Road because Kent's got a girl friend over there somewhere. Anyway, they got into a discussion and I guess it heated up. Kent slugged Pete. Kent throws a hell of a punch." He stopped for breath and pounded his fist into his palm. "Wasn't the first time. But you know that."

Hetty swallowed and managed to nod.

"Thing is, our Saint Peter had a way of getting in the middle, didn't he? Kent says the first time they got into it was back when Pete wanted him to confess to his bride about some lady friend." Johnny shrugged and sighed. "Saint Pete was a great believer in the truth, the whole truth and nothing but the truth, wasn't he? 'Why don't you just sit down and level with her,' he said and Kent said he just...lost it."

He thought for a minute. "Lost Delia, too, didn't he? How long were they married? About six months?"

"About."

Johnny sat and looked at her, cracking his knuckles, grinning uneasily. "Thing is, Kent slugged him."

His words were beginning to sound slushy.

Hetty realized that her hands were shaking. She tucked them beneath her elbows.

"So that's what happened out there," Johnny said. "Peter probably came up with one of his little gems, playing God, and Kent hauled off and popped him one." He refilled his glass.

Hetty gazed at the scrubbed surface of the table, remembering Peter's bruised and swollen face in that unit.

"I see," she said.

"It's Kent's truck." Johnny took a long swallow and lifted the bottle toward her glass. "Top you off?" When she shook her head he poured himself another and sat back.

"So. It was Kent," she said, her voice paper thin. "Kent. And the whole thing was actually a kind of accident?"

Johnny lifted his glass and put it down. He made a series of wet rings on the table and interlocked them. "Thing is, none of us want Kent to go to prison," he said. "Do we? Not for a—it had to be just a wild punch. A kind of an accident, yeah."

Hetty looked at her hands. Were those her hands?

"He's so scared. Poor guy bought a gun. A Smith and Wesson thirty-eight. Dave and I found out about it and we figured he might want to kill himself with it so I took it away from him."

He was beginning to talk too fast. "Well, I didn't exactly take it away from him. I bought the damned thing from him. Poor guy never has enough money to last him to the first of the month. I'm not sure he bought it in the first place. I think maybe he took it away from some kid out in the parking lot behind the school, and—and you don't believe a damned bit of this, do you, kid?"

Hetty tried to shake her head.

"I'll show you," he said. "I've got that little thirty-eight in my glove compartment. Paid Kent a hundred bucks for the thing. Shoots five rounds. It's kind of pretty. You want to see it?"

She didn't.

He went to the door, yanked it open, lurched out in the rain and came hurrying back in, his big head pulled down between his shoulders, a revolver in his hand. "Said he took this away from some high school kid, you believe it?" He passed the gun back and forth in his big hands. "May not be worth a hundred bucks but I figured he can use the money. What the hell. You want it? Here. It's yours. A birthday present. Put it in your night stand."

Hetty couldn't look away. She sat very still. She wanted to say, "Put that away," but she couldn't. Her mouth couldn't form words.

"Aw, why would I want to hurt our Pete?" he whispered, tears glittering in his eyes.

He finished what was in his glass and refilled it. "Ah, hell," he said. "The whole damned mess started when Emily went to see him. Peter. And he told her he'd talk to me. Make me see the light.

The light according to Saint Peter. Big authority on how I'm supposed to treat my only daughter. He had her riding around with that yahoo on that Harley, with a bunch of cutthroats. What gave him the right to wreck my little girl's life?" He grimaced, fighting tears. "Poor, crazy, damn' bastard, why couldn't he just tell her to come on home and talk to me?"

He shook his head, his mouth twisting. "Had to tell her she's got a right to choose her own life. What does that mean? 'Choose your own life?' Does that mean take up with any dope head with a flashy motorcycle? 'Choose your own life.' He probably worked in a little poetry."

When Johnny could talk again, the words came through sobbing half breaths. "Emily came home and said she had been talking to him. To Saint Peter. My girl."

It made him choke. He got up and walked over and stood with his brow against the pane of the window beside the back door. "She went to that classroom and talked to him and came home and started packing her bags. I've lost everything. Every damned thing I ever wanted." He bumped his brow against the edge of the window. "Pete did that to me. That's what he did. To me. To us. That's what he did."

Hetty forced herself to be still, to focus on the rivulets of water coursing down the window pane. Rain was seeping in at one edge of the pane, puddling on the sill. It must not have been the first time this window had leaked in that way. There was a place where the paint had flaked off, a bared oval in the ivory paint where the water built up and rounded, nearing the edge of the sill. She concentrated on watching the water bulge, as Johnny's voice went on.

"His story," he was saying, his voice rasping. "Her story. My story. What the hell." He hit the edge of the sill with the heel of his hand. "Son-of-a-bitch. I never meant to knock him out, let alone kill him. But who'll believe that?"

He walked to the sink and came back to stand near Hetty, cracking his knuckles. "It's killing Hallie. She's—Hallie can't handle it. She's sick. Emily, my girl, my little girl." His laugh sounded strangled. "We haven't seen her since Pete's funeral. We've lost her. I don't even know where she is." His shoulders shook. "What made him so damn sure he could tell us how to live?"

The puddle on the window sill broke through. It began to trickle over the edge of the sill. Hetty got up intending to get a cloth to mop it up, but it wasn't worth the effort. She sat back down.

"It was a fucking accident," Johnny said. He drew in a long, uneven breath. "I didn't even mean to hit him, don't you get it? Why couldn't you leave it alone? Why did you have to keep at it and keep at it. If I go to prison, it'll kill Hallie, don't you see that? It'll kill her. I can't let that happen."

Hetty unclasped her hands and turned them over. She focused on her palm, on the faint line that palm readers call the lifeline, a curving crease from the bottom of her hand to between her first finger and thumb. She flexed her palm to watch the meaty part in front of her thumb lift and pucker.

"Peter listened," Hetty said, her voice stronger now. "Should he have refused to listen? Would you have had him turn away? He listened. That's what Peter did. He did it well. He listened to her that Friday afternoon, in his classroom. And then, when you called, he listened to you. And he listened to you when you wanted to see him, to talk to him. I can hear him. 'You're losing her because you're hanging on too tight.' Is that what he said? Should he have turned away? Should he have been silent? 'The cruelest lies are often told in silence.'"

"Sounds like him," Johnny said.

"Yes," she said. "Yes, it does."

Johnny turned and walked clumsily into the hall. He bumped into the frame of the door. When he turned back to face her and stood leaning against the wall, Hetty thought, suddenly sick with terror, why, he's going to shoot me.

"No," she told him but Johnny, the gun glinting in his hand, peered at her, his big head swaying, his voice mournful, saying, "Aw, Hetty, honey, damn it all."

24

"No," Hetty said. "You mustn't."

The kitchen door thumped. Bang, bang, bang.

The door slammed open and Peg came stamping in with a wet grocery bag coming apart in her hands, shaking rivers of rain from a dripping umbrella. She looked at Hetty, whirled around to look at Johnny with the gun in his hand--

--gasped, "Holy shit!" She dropped the bag and umbrella on the floor and tripped over them.

Johnny made a strange, snorting, strangled sound.

Hetty grabbed her purse from the corner table and pushed at Peg as she stumbled to her feet. "What?" Peg squealed. "What?"

"Run," Hetty yelled. She yanked the kitchen door open so hard it hit the wall and bounced. She fell against Peg, shoving at her, shouting, "Run!"

They ran, stumbling, bumping into each other, across the slippery lawn, to Clara in the driveway.

Hetty got Clara's door unlocked. She was trying to wrench it open as Johnny came out and stood on the walk outside the back door with his feet wide apart, both his hands out in front of him, his left hand supporting his right, aiming the gun.

The gun flashed and exploded.

A burst of wind shoved at Hetty, slamming her face down in the wet grass. She staggered to her knees and leaned above the concrete edge of the driveway, astonished at the sight of a small neat drop of blood, and another. Her shoulder seemed to be oozing. I'm shot, she thought, and, since it didn't hurt, it took another explosion and a singing whine over Clara's hood to make her believe it.

Peggy gasped. "My God. You're bleeding. What's he doing?"

"Get in," Hetty shouted.

A bullet slammed into Clara's side with a solid heavy thunk and Hetty said to herself, her mind actually forming the words, *oh, good car. Solid car.*

She got Clara's door open, scrambled in, slid and fell over as Peg slid in behind her. "You have to drive," Hetty gasped. "Here. Key."

Peg clambered over her and cowered behind the steering wheel. "I can't," she bleated. "I can't drive this thing."

"Try," Hetty said, wheezing. "Try." She didn't seem to have any right arm. There was nothing, an emptiness, where her arm ought to be. Pounding at it didn't help. She sprawled on the floor mat below the front seat, hoarsely begging Peg to drive, drive, go.

She rose up high enough to see Johnny coming across the lawn, running, his face grotesque. He got to the window on her side of the car and stared in at them, rain washing down his face, half his big face widened into mouth as he howled, leaning against the window and then beating at it, beating with his fist and the gun. He backed off and held the gun up, aiming at Peg, at Hetty, Hetty thinking *now I am going to die,* shaking, shaking, sliding under the dash as far as she could get.

Johnny slammed the butt of the gun against the glass. It didn't break. He jerked the car door open, loomed above Hetty, holding the long part of the gun, the barrel, in his fist, drawing his hand up and back, grimacing, swinging the gun up—

--as Peg screamed and stamped on the accelerator. Clara started up with a roar. They lurched down the drive. "I can't work this thing," Peg screamed. "How do you work this thing?"

Hetty found the clutch, saying, "Down. Down." She moved the stick shift into low gear, holding it with her good hand and arm, with her entire self, shifting Clara into first gear and, as Peg obeyed, getting Clara into second, Hetty grinding her teeth, Clara grinding her gears.

Clara bucked out into the street. Hetty's hand kept sliding off the pedal. The engine died. Hetty scrambled and fell into a better position, got the gear shift back into her slippery fist, Peg saying, "I can't," over and over.

"Give it gas," Hetty screamed. "You can."

Peg stamped on the accelerator. Hetty shoved, leaning, panting. Clara coughed into life. They went jerking down the street.

Clara's engine died.

They did it again, the two of them wrestling Clara into first, clumsily into second and third and, finally, Clara's poor tired engine groaning gravelly protests, into high gear. "Don't stop," Hetty gasped, falling back, trying to roll out of Peg's way, clutching at her dead shoulder, as Clara jerked and faltered, sped up and jerked, bumping along, Peg driving, driving, swearing and praying, up Sagewick. They skidded around a turn.

"Sabo," Peg yelled. "Oh, God, the ditch."

"Don't stop," Hetty said. "My hands won't work."

"Shit!" Peg said, "Who's stopping? I'm floor boarding it."

Hetty could see that, yes, there was Peg's foot, in its black and white striped, untied, Vans shoe, flat against Clara's black rubber mat.

Horn blasts backed up Peg's prayers and curses. "Shit, shit, oh God, oh hell," she shrieked as she leaned and swayed. "Sagemont" and, "Kirkmont" and then, "Here he comes! Right behind us."

Hetty couldn't see anything. Then she could. They rounded a corner and she fell up into the seat, her eyes and throat burning with tears and terror, her right shoulder and arm convulsing in such sudden exquisite pain that her entire left side contracted.

Waves of water splattered the windshield and windows. They careened into a muddy field, orange barrels clattering, flying up and away. Men flashed up in front of them, and scrambled out of the way.

At the end of the field a white and orange wall had a tall shining ladder leading to a luminous azure heaven. Hetty saw it, clear as clear. A heavenly ladder leading to heaven.

For one wild, silent, eerie moment the rungs of the ladder shone close, closer, as the ladder hung before them, gleaming, going up, up a rounded orange and white wall into an opening in the clouds, into an azure sky.

Clara slid and slammed and exploded. The world went black.

Hetty snorted. A piece of metal tore at her chin. A pedal. She couldn't seem to get her legs unkinked. Not enough room. She peeled a small, smelly, torn, fragment of rubber away from her nose and her nose started running, hurting so violently that it began, of its own volition, to make sad snerfling noises. She put out her hand to brush at the floor in front of her face and stopped, at once. The floor was covered with glittering sharp shards swirling in iridescent fluid and what must surely be blood. Her blood?

"Peg?" she said. "Where are you?"

Peg was gone. The door hung open on Peg's side of the car. Hetty could see pavement, black pavement and smoke, but no Peg. Peg had to be there somewhere.

A man's round face appeared at the window above Hetty. He yanked at Clara's door. Another man joined the first. Clara's crushed door made terrible wrenching noises and fell away. The splinters of glass on the floor eddied. The men yelled, "Dummy lee mano," shouting, wanting her to do something. "Dummy lee mano," they grunted, dragging her from beneath the steering column and Clara's caved-in dashboard.

Hetty pushed at them and stood up. "Peg?" She gasped.

The men wanted her to hurry. Hetty ran, leaning on the men, lurching on rubbery legs, saying, "Look. Wait. Where are my shoes?" trying not to step on stones, rough places in the pavement.

The three of them staggered across a gravelly area, both men breathing hoarsely. One of them kept wanting to pick her up but she spat and swallowed, pushing at him, palming blood from her eyes, running, bumping along, a surprising amount of salty blood in her mouth and all down her drenched blouse.

The men didn't want her to have to run any more, but they seemed frantically emphatic about not staying too near Clara. Clara seemed to have become part of the vast rounded side of a cement mixer. Clara's tires, black puddles, kept exploding, imploding, sending flames up the rounded wall.

They reached the edge of the pavement and stopped, inhaling smoke. One of the men wanted her to sit down. She was contemplating this, queasily wondering how best to go about bending her knees and letting go so that she might sink to the ground. The air had gone eerily silent again, a thick silence, forcing its way into her ears. She couldn't seem to get balanced. She put out her hand, the one that still had feeling in it, as the muddy ground came up to meet her. The black at the edges of world closed in.

The darkness became a kind of fog in a bouncing tin room, a sleeper, a small metal sleeping room on a train, a Pullman. No. An ambulance. A careening ambulance. Hetty wanted, fervently, to tell the driver to not go so fast, please, but where was he? "Speed kills," she said, and there was Peg, with gory scratches on her dirty face, bouncing along, sitting next to a crouching policeman, oh, wonderful Peg, wonderfully there, frantic and crazy. "Are you hurt?" Hetty asked.

Peg shoved at her matted hair. "I don't know," she said, crying. "I don't think so."

"How can you not be hurt?" Hetty said.

"I don't know," Peg said. "I don't know. Clean living?" She jiggled against the policeman. and peered at him demanding, "what the hell do you think you're doing? Are you writing a *ticket?*"

"I guess," the policeman said, distractedly. "Was she driving?"

"She's been shot," Peg said. "Can't you see?"

"Shot?" The policeman fell against Peg. "Lady," he said to Hetty, "Who shot you?"

"Excuse me?" A man in a white suit had Hetty's arm in his hand; her good arm, the one with a plastic tube embedded beneath a bandage on it, taped to a padded board. He was dispassionately relaying numbers, talking to himself, smiling down at Hetty. He leaned close, a tag on his shirt close to Hetty's nose. "Caduceus," Hetty said. "Oh, Peg, you're really all right?"

Peg cried harder.

"Johnny?" Hetty asked.

"He's okay," Peg said. "He's got his own ambulance."

The man in the starchy white shirt moved closer, edging Peg and the policeman out of his way. Peg's blotchy face jiggled and tilted. The policeman seemed to be trying to write on a tablet on his knee. The white-shirted man pressed cold gauze to Hetty's nose, his voice low, repeating something that Hetty couldn't comprehend. Her shoulder and arm had gone away again but her nose hurt frantically. A plastic bag with a smear of blood on it swung wildly from a fastener on a chrome metal rail in the ceiling. "Talk to me," the man in white said. "I'm the paramedic here."

"What would you like to discuss?" Hetty asked him, nasally.

"Atta girl," the man said.

"Were you shot?" the policeman asked. "Lady?"

"Shoes and ships and sealing wax," Hetty told the paramedic. "Cabbages and kings."

"Yesss!" the man said.

"Who shot you?" the policeman said. He sounded tearful.

Hetty focused on the paramedic. "And sure the poet spewed up a good lump of clotted nonsense," she said, trying not to cry.

He smiled down at her. "Sounds right to me," he said. "You'll do."

"Nose, nose," Hetty wept, "jolly red nose. Nutmegs and cinnamon."

"All right," the tech said, his smile broadening. "Nice going."

"Yes." Hetty swallowed. The man had fireflies around his face.

"Got some radiator fluid on yourself," he told her. His teeth shone through the sparkling insects. "Must be what's keeping you so cool. Tell you what, lady. You'll do."

Having the paramedic say she was cool was heartening. Concentrating on that helped Hetty to get back some control. "A pobble's toes are safe," she told him, "provided he sees to his nose. Don' t cry, Peggy." Peg's eyes glittered through smoky smudges.

"Talk to me," the man said. "Don't leave me."

"Mustn't nag," Hetty said, through her teeth. Couldn't he see she was trying? Her shoulder had come screaming back. She had two shoulders again. Two agonized shoulders and a cramping right arm. "Oh, Charley," she gritted, gasping, "Horse. Charley horse. My shoulder. Is. Bent. Wrong." Her arm and shoulder convulsed, squeezing, squeezing tighter.

But it was her nose, it was her poor torn, freezing, stopped up, screaming nose, that *hurt.*

25

Hetty's feverish nose sent urgent fierce signals pulsing through the stuff the nurses kept shooting into her. During one of the intervals when she was awake, she looked over at Peg and whispered, "Johnny?"

Peg was silent for so long that Hetty came out of her daze and her stomach gave a lurch.

She knew, even before Peg shook her head. "Did he die quickly?"

"He never made it to the hospital."

"Oh," Hetty said, weeping, "What's to become of Hallie, now? And Emily? Oh, Peg. Johnny. I can't bear it."

"Don't," Peg said. "I won't cry anymore if you don't."

*

At dawn, Hetty's shoulder had settled into a cold dull ache but her heavy, fat, stopped-up nose sent out exquisite lightning jabs of pain and all her insides kept cramping. The pain brought her whimpering up from the bottom of a velvety dreamless sea. She hurt so it was hard to breathe. Trays clattered out in the hall. Hetty heard herself making all sorts of noises and stopped at once because George Gordon sat across from her, all caved in on himself, slumped in a chair with his brow against the metal foot of her bed.

"Angel," he said.

"You look as though you ought to be in that bed over there," Hetty croaked.

"Angel," he said again. He came around to her side and kissed her on the cheek and her brow.

"Could you not look so awful, please?" Hetty said.

"It's that ghastly scent of disinfectant," he said. "Never could abide the way hospitals smell. And the coffee is unbelievable." He embarked on a series of vigorous noises meant to mask a sob. "Oh, my," he whimpered. "Oh, honey, your pretty face. Couldn't you have landed on your backside?"

Hetty couldn't help groaning.

"You're going to be just fine," George Gordon said, his eyes wild with alarm. "That's my girl. Fine as silk."

"Yes," Hetty said. "Can't talk." Her shoulder had a hard toothache. It seethed. The sunlit room had a tall metal bed over across the way, with a pastel painting of a silly, overblown, white and purple lily hanging next to it and a green and white blanket folded at its foot. Oh, Clara, Hetty thought foggily, where am I going to find another green and white Clara?

A stately black nurse came in holding aloft a hypodermic syringe.

The next time she swam into consciousness it was noon, Peg said. Peg wanted her to look at whatever was emitting a fetid odor from beneath the turquoise cover of an insulated lunch tray. Hetty suggested she cover the tray back up at once and Peg went running out to the nursing station, A nurse came in, with a blessed shot.

There was one after that and then the pain settled down to a bearable rhythm and the room was dimly lit and there was Peg, again, balancing a long, flimsy, white baker's box full of eclairs that she said were for the nurses. "I gave a couple to your lieutenant and his friend," she said. "They're waiting out there for you to sober up and quit talking about pobbles. What's a pobble? Good hell, you look awful."

"Thank you," Hetty said. "What day is it? You look pretty awful, yourself. And if you were literate at all you'd know about pobbles."

"I don't doubt it," Peg said. "If I look awful it's got to be your fault. You make me crazy. I'm going to have to find a more sane and healthy class of friends."

"We both are," Hetty said.

"Yes," Peg said. Her face went grim. "Aw, hell, Hetty."

"Yes," Hetty said. "Johnny," she whispered.

They were still tearful when the nurses let Lieutenant Gray come in. He looked wretchedly uncomfortable. He stood next to the bed, gazing at Hetty for several minutes before he asked, gently, in his chocolate voice, "Do you feel like talking?"

"She's dead drunk," Peg said. "We might be talking about pobbles, here."

"I see," he said.

"You know anything much about pobbles?" Peg said.

A smile flickered across the lieutenant's face. "I do."

"Why am I not surprised," Peg said. "Just the same, can't this wait? It's all over, anyway, now, isn't it? Give her a chance to heal, can't you?"

"Peg," Hetty said. "Talk less."

She put out her good hand for the lieutenant to take in his warm hand. "A certain amount of discomfort shouldn't flumboozle a person," she said. She gazed at the painting across the way. The flower in the small square kept growing and shrinking, as if it were alive, like a Harry Potter picture. She kept watching it as some part of her realized that she must try to explain, now. She had to make Tom Gray, make everyone, comprehend Johnny's agony at losing his beautiful Emily.

"What if," she began, and stopped. The flower shivered and shrank. "Once upon a time," she said, starting over, "a good man, a loving and decent man, a man who never had struck anyone in anger in all his days, struck his friend." Her throat ached, but she had to go on. "The friend that he hit might not have meant to provoke him. He might have been brimming with love but, you see, he found the wrong word." She paused. The flower in the square on the wall was ballooning, again. She sighed. "He let loose the wrong word. Like the blue string on a cat food bag? He made everything fall open. He loosed a storm of rage. And the gentle man hit his friend as hard as he could. He couldn't help it." She tried to clear her head. "The gentle man had all this agony and he put it in his fist and smashed it against his friend."

Lieutenant Gray's eyes squeezed closed. When he opened them he was saying something to her but she couldn't quite hear him.

Hetty tugged at his hand so he would lean closer. "I could try again," she whispered. "I'm afraid I'm a total loss."

"Ah," the lieutenant said, close to her ear. "You'll do."

After the lieutenant left, George Gordon walked in with a huge bouquet. He dropped it on a chair and hurried to the side of the bed. "Angel?" he said, his blue eyes blazing with alarm. "What are these people doing to you?"

He was effusively relieved when Peg told him that they had been discussing Johnny. "Ah," he said. "Poor devil." A bit later he looked at Hetty through his shaggy eyebrows. "How did you know he was the one?"

"He lied," Hetty said. "He kept lying." She was growing tired of explaining. "Even when he wasn't talking, he lied. That's when he lied the most." She put her head back on her pillows. "'The cruelest lies are often told in silence.'"

"She's quoting Peter," George Gordon said to Peg.

Hetty nodded. "Can't you hear him? I do, all the time."

*

During Peg's next visit, Hetty suggested she take some of the flowers crowded on the windowsill and along the wall home with her.

"You ought to see my house, " Peg said. "Boxes and boxes, all over the place." She sighed happily, went over to the empty bed on the other side of the room and bounced down on it. "Now that you're making sense, again—as much as you ever do, I mean—have I got news or have I got news." She swung her legs. "There's this woman has people putting little blue and green flowers and golden birth dates on these ceramic baby shoes. She's made a small fortune but her husband's gone to Florida and she's getting tired of running the business so she wants to get rid of it." She had to stop to catch her breath. "Get rid of the fever so they'll let you out of here. You and I are going into the china baby shoe business."

Peg slid off the bed to pace and tug at her hair. "I was thinking about becoming a dispatcher at the cop shop before this woman came along. Doris Gofor's telling everybody that she's looking for someone to train as a police dispatcher for the cop shop. I thought about applying but I don't think she thinks I'm much of a candidate. Who'd want to do that, anyway?" She shrugged. "Oh, and you know what else? Some gossip. One of your friends in the water color society is supposed to have murdered her husband. Everybody is buzzing about it. This woman's husband called nine-one-one for help because his wife was killing him only his wife was across town getting a ticket for driving too slow on the Katy freeway, so how could she have?" Peg was so wound up that she kept bouncing.

"That detective," she said, "the lieutenant, don't you think he looks sort of like Richard—"

"No," Hetty said. Her shoulder pulsed. Richard Dreyfuss swam into view, up near the ceiling, in the misty corner. The lieutenant did, in a way, have something of Richard Dreyfuss about him. But he looked like himself, of course.

Peg didn't leave until a nurse came in to give Hetty a shot that sent her sliding off the edge of the world.

*

On Wednesday morning a cricket chirping somewhere in the room brought Hetty fully awake. She propped herself up on her good elbow and listened, bemused, wondering how a cricket could get to the third floor of a hospital and where it could be hiding on such an immaculate, seamless expanse of floor. She couldn't see the thing but it stayed, chirping insect barks or possibly they were meant to be invitations.

She was peering around at the floor, trying to see the insect, when a florist's delivery woman came in bearing another plant, one in a slotted pot with little white roots sticking out all around. It had seven tiny, perfect, pale, freckled orchids clinging to a long, curved, spindly stem. The card had a monogrammed signature in a Dutch shoe: "C.V.H."

At ten o'clock a small, irascible, pink-nosed surgeon strode briskly in to examine Hetty's wound, which was very sore. He was too busy for a lot of explaining but it seems the rotator cuff and various muscles had been damaged, but there oughtn't to have been so much pain. The shoulder would require extensive therapy. And all this was because she, Hetty, had led him down a garden path.

Being led down a garden path made the man very cranky.

Hetty hadn't been aware of doing any leading down any garden paths. She smiled up at the man, seeing herself harvesting cut flowers, roses and delphinium, mischievously gamboling in a whimsical garden, too busy putting cut flowers in a basket to realize that she'd strayed from the hospital entirely and that he was following along, with his eyes so annoyed they were becoming brown rectangles under his beetling brow.

"You've had an infection," the surgeon said, as if she did it on purpose, just to worry him.

Hetty said she truly hoped too many of his patients wouldn't lead him down too many garden paths.

The man suggested she might want to go home.

Oh, home.

Peg and George Gordon came to fetch her.

As she was wheeled through the hospital's sliding doors, Hetty lifted her bandaged face to the low slanting light of the November sun and said, fervently, "Oh, how good."

George Gordon beamed approval. "That's my warm, wise, wonderful, beautiful angel, the light of my life," he said, "the loveliest—"

"Oh, Dad," Hetty murmured, "That will do." Then, remembering Lieutenant Gray's hesitant smile and the emergency technician's voice, in that bouncing ambulance, she added, quietly, to herself, "I'll do."

"Do what?" Peg asked.

Hetty smiled. "All kinds of things," she said. "You'll see."